THORNY PILSUDSKI

&

THE GIRL IN THE BEEMER

BY

STEVEN SCHWARTZ

ALSO BY STEVEN SCHWARTZ

A TRIO OF TALES: THREE NOVELLAS

INTO THE LIFE

UNTETHERED

TOMMY GUN BLUES & LUCAS

THE SHARPENED QUILL (EDITOR)

GUMSHOE A GO-GO

THE CHEEKY MONKEY

THORNY PILSUDSKI

&

THE GIRL IN THE BEEMER

BY

STEVEN SCHWARTZ

A SHADOW PRESS BOOK

All the characters in this book are fictitious.
Any resemblance to actual persons living or
dead is purely coincidental and not intended
by the author

Book design by Ariel Louiselle

Published by Shadow Press

DEDICATION

To the city of Chicago and all its strange and fascinating characters. It was a wonderful place to grow up in. It has provided me with enough stories to last a lifetime.

PART ONE

ONE

The sound of the wound up four banger
coming at me was unmistakable. I leapt back
onto the curb as a red BMW 2002 Bavaria
careened around the corner and onto
Lawrence Avenue. I had just enough time
and the beam from a handy streetlight to
catch a glimpse of the long haired blonde at
the wheel. She had cut her wheel so hard on
the turn that the car nearly went into a four
wheel drift. Hot on her tail was a squad car.
Its Mars lights were flashing like a go-go
dancer doing the funky chicken. Its siren was
screaming like a dame in a Hammer horror
film. I and the small crowd that stood
outside the just closed Green Mill jazz club
in Uptown Chicago cheered the runaway
dame on. It was a 2 in the AM free show for
all us zonked out beboppers, dopers, and
jazz heads.

I and my half in the bag wasted pals stood laying odds on her chances of outrunning the fuzz. We were all either drunk, stoned, or just fried from too much music, too much dancing, and way too much drinking. It was late and the night was steamy. The August air was rife with humidity. The smell from the evaporating water just sprayed by a passing sanitation truck coupled with the natural stink of the oil-slick city streets filled our heads. It was the unmistakable smell of a hot night in the big city of Chicago. I loved it.

We debated heading for an after hours place we knew of down the block. The consensus came out in the negative. I said goodbye to my pals and the sleepy-eyed gals hanging on to them. I headed around the corner to find my wheels in the Uptown Theaters parking lot. I had no trouble spotting my battered blue and white 54 Chevy. It was the only car and the only sign of life left in the lot, or so I thought. As I approached my hunk of rusty Detroit iron I turned my head in every direction. A lot of junkies and other bad apples roamed the white trash infested neighborhood. I had a penlight in one hand and my other hand was on the butt of the snub-nosed .38 holstered handle forward on my left hip. As a P.I., I had a license to carry. The lot seemed deserted. I let go of my pistol and fished out my car keys. I inserted the key into my car door when I heard a low whistle. I let go of the keys and pulled out my .38. I looked around. A dumpster stood at the back of the lot. The low whistle came again. I slowly walked towards the sound. I flashed my small light around the back of the refuse container and there she was. It was the blonde from the Beemer. She grinned up at me.

"You see any cops out there?" she said, looking up at me.

She stood up. She looked to be in her late 20's or maybe a well preserved 30 something. She had on a green dress and low heels. Her long hair framed a round face with a wide nose and huge almost black eyes. Her pearly whites shone in the glare of my small light. She stood about 5 feet 5 and was distributed about as a well as a woman could be distributed.

"Hey, douse the light. I don't need anyone spotting us here."

I shut off the penlight. "That was some turn you made back there. You take lessons from Stirling Moss?"

"Who is that? Never mind. How about you give me a lift to where I dumped my car. The coast should clear by now. Jesus, these cops are everywhere. You figure this time of night I wouldn't get hassled."

I laughed. "Two in the AM, you're speeding down Broadway, and you wonder why the cops are after you? What else they got to do at this hour?"

"I dunno'," she said. "Maybe eat doughnuts and roust darkies."

"I think they do that all the time. Chasing a hot dame in a German Go-Cart is a novelty for the boys in blue."

She stepped out from behind the dumpster. She walked around in front of me. The dim glow from the distant streetlight was enough for her to get a good look at me. I grinned. She grinned.

"Hey, you're kinda' cute. How about we get my car later. Wanna' catch some sounds and have a drink. I know a place."

"Am I correct in thinking you are talking about the black unmarked door about two blocks from here? The one where they slide open a slot and you got to be known by Linko or it's a no-go?"

She laughed. "That's the place. How is it I've never seen you there?"

"Maybe the same reason I never saw you there. Or maybe I did and don't remember."

"Honey, you would remember if you saw me. I ain't the kind of girl a guy forgets; or so I've been told. It must be this."

She reached up and removed the blonde wig. Her dark hair was pinned up. She shook it loose. She reached in her purse. She stuffed the wig inside. She pulled out a pair of glasses and put them on.

"Shit, it's you," I said. "Sure, I've seen you. Hard to not see someone who moves on the dance floor like you do. What's with the wig? New look? Pulling a job? On the lamb? Maybe wanted in all 48 states? Think I could turn you in for a juicy reward?"

She eyed me with a frown on her face. "Look, let's get out of here before the cops return."

"Fine by me. Maybe you got a reward for me better than the one the fuzz might be offering."

"Jesus, but ain't you the wise guy. I am not wanted by any cops, at least not that I know of. What about you? You a bad boy or just a little late night lamb that has lost its way?"

"How about we compare notes and tell lies over a couple of drinks?"

She smiled. I smiled. We got in my car. I drove around the block a couple of times to make sure we were not being followed. We spotted her car parked between a large van and a tireless wreck. I made my way back to Lawrence Avenue. I parked a block from the Dew Drop Inn behind the Paradise Theater. I shut off the car. I turned to her.

"My name is Thornell Pilsudski. People call me Thorny. And you are?"

"Well, that's a mouthful. I'm Myra Rosebush. Before you ask and they always ask, I am half black and half Crow Indian. I take it you are some sort of half-breed yourself. I get the Polish moniker but not the first half."

"Oh, you mean the Thornell. My father was a huge jazz fan. I'm named after a guitar player. I take it you like jazz."

"Like it? I love it. I've seen them all. You know, Bird, Dizzy, and all them cats. That's why I like going to Linko's. You never know who might show up and sit in after their gigs."

I smiled at my good fortune. "I can't believe it. I meet a beautiful woman in the middle of the night and she turns out to be an Indian jazz fan with a mysterious past and a Nazi speedster. I must be living right."

I got out of the car and went around to her side. I opened the door and helped her out of the car. I shut her door with a few pops and squeaks coming from the old heap.

"Don't get all warmed up, Thorny," she said. "Last time I checked we had yet to be written up as an item in Kup's column. How about you tamp down the budding romance stuff and let's get upstairs before Linko throws everybody out."

"Reet Poteet, Sugar. Drinks on me."

"Well, ain't you the gentleman Jim. Buying a girl a drink. How gallant. What; you normally don't buy your girls drinks?"

I smiled. "Not always. Sometimes it pays to play hard to get. I don't want to be thought of as some round-heeled pushover."

Now she laughed. "Not to worry, Buster. No smootching on first dates, if that's what this is. I am not sure; you tell me."

"Sweetheart, I would not tell you anything. You look like a smart dame. Figure it out yourself and when you do then tell me. Come on, let's head up and cut a rug while I'm still awake and able to move."

She threw her big beautiful head back and started to laugh.

"Cut a rug, indeed. Now ain't you a high school throwback. I haven't heard that one in a long time."

"Probably a lot you ain't heard," I said. "But you stick with me and you'll hear a lot more. This daddy-o knows 'em all."

TWO

I knocked on an unmarked black door that was set back off the sidewalk. After a few seconds a panel in the upper part of the door slid open. Linko's fat face appeared. He scoped us up and down. He smiled. At least I think he smiled. It is hard to tell with all that blubber vibrating on his unshaven face. The door swung open and his chubby fingers motioned for us to head upstairs. I could hear a slow blues beat being pounded out on the bass along with some soaring sax sounds. I followed Myra's well-formed and deliciously gyrating rear end up and into the main room. A few scattered tables were spread around the sparse room. A make-shift bar stood at one end of the room. A small bandstand was placed against a far wall. Two couples were wobbling around the space between the tables. I wasn't sure if they were dancing or just holding each other up. Not that it mattered much at this hour. Tucked into one corner was a skinny guy talking to a flaming redhead. He looked lost and she looked mean as hell. It was the usual late night crowd that found its way to this unlicensed and mob owned after hours dive.

I got us a couple of highballs from the bar. We took a sip. I pulled Myra up and we joined the swaying group on the floor. She felt good to the touch. She felt right and damn if she didn't smell more than right. I could not identify the perfume but it was a scent I wouldn't soon forget. I spotted Linko in the corner watching us. Or more accurately watching her. I could never figure out if Linko owned the place, just kept things cool, or exactly what the deal was. Of course this was Chicago in the 60's. It was either the Mob, the cops, or the city that ran everything. They all deftly avoided stepping on each others toes but as a P.I. I had to walk a fine line between all of them. Asking the wrong question of the wrong person could lead to disastrous results. One of these results could be a quick exit from the land of the living. I found that out the hard way. I grew up in this town and I thought I knew my way around. I was in for some big surprises. After a few years of chasing errant hubbies, finding runaways, and the odd occasional insurance scam track-down, I figured I was pretty well in on the basic who's who. I was to find out that I had a lot more to learn. But right now, right here, all I wanted to learn was the combination to unlocking the door to Myra's hidden treasures.

We twirled and swayed. I looked deep into her dark eyes and got flutters in my nether regions. Normally I am a bit cautious when it comes to strange dames but this pulchritudinous Pocahontas, despite my utter exhaustion, had got my juices flowing like Niagara Falls during the spring thaw.

We sat down. We drank. A few people waved at Myra. They were not the kind of people one takes home to Mother. A small shiver of doubt fluttered its way across my chest. Was this little injun connected? Was she in any way legit? Who was I kidding? Your upstanding citizen had no knowledge of joints like this. I had questions but I feared they might put her off. And besides; who wasn't connected to something or someone in this town? Hell, two doors away was a mob owned pool hall above the theater. I went up there once just to check it out and see if I knew anyone. I was told it was run by an old mob enforcer and a good place to gather info for a price. A few years ago I took a shot and I climbed the stairs to the upper floor. I spotted an old guy seated behind a glass counter. I looked around at the dark smoky room. There were eight tables and all of them were in use. I spotted some local muscle and the usual array of needle freaks, B and E boys, and general miscreants. The old guy behind the counter caught my eye. He shook his head at me and looked toward the stairs I had just climbed. I got the message. I left and have never gone back. He obviously knew something that I didn't. What it was is probably something I was better off not knowing.

We finished our drinks. The quartet took a break. Myra tapped my hand.

"Nobody big here tonight. These cats are OK but nothing special. How about we blow this pop stand? I'm ready for some shut eye. I'm going back to my car and head home."

"I know what you mean. How about we go to my place? Or if you think that's too risky, then how about your place?"

She looked at me. "You expect a lot for a short ride. How about we get to know each other a little before we do anything drastic."

Linko was still watching her. "Hey, you realize that Linko never takes his eyes off you? You friends or something?"

She laughed. She turned and waved at the fat man. He waved back. "We go back some," she said. "He likes to look out for me. He's also a sort of pipeline to certain people."

"That sounds interesting. Am I to assume that you may not be 100 per cent legit?"

Her face got rigid. "You can assume anything you like, Thorny. But chances are it will be wrong."

"Well, how about you set me straight. Who am I escorting out of here this morning?"

"No more questions."

She reached in her purse. She took out a pen. She scribbled something on a napkin.

"Here's my number. Give me a call and we can pick this up later. I'm gonna' do a little business. Linko will get me safe to my car. Don't you worry. Give me a call. I might even answer."

She got up and went through a door that I had not noticed before. Linko wiggled out of his chair and pushed himself erect. His raspy voice boomed out.

"That's it folks. No more band or booze. Time to shut it down. See youse guys tomorrow night. Don't forget the tip jar for the band."

As I shuffled my way out Linko grabbed me. "You be nice to her, you hear. She's special and means a lot to someone you don't want to mess with."

I pulled my arm away. "Ease up, Linko. I only met her tonight. The cops were chasing her and I gave her a ride here. I don't know anything about her. Just what am I not in on here? Who is she?"

"If she wants you to know things then she will tell you. Just a friendly word, that's all."

"Got ya', big man. I'm cool."

I descended the steps. I left the night behind and entered the brutal soul-destroying daylight. It was already hot, humid, and sticky. My skin was dried out from all the booze. My clothes felt scratchy and I was in a bad mood. The sun had risen over Lake Michigan and hung low in the sky. It was a blazing smog shrouded ball of heat. I had to blink my eyes against the glare. I pulled a pair of shades from my inside pocket. I put them on. My eyes sent me a big thanks. I stumbled my way to my beater Chevy. It had no AC and was so hot inside that if I had a couple of eggs handy I could have cooked my breakfast on the hood. I drove north to my apartment. It was hard getting the smell of her out of my head. I could still feel her firm thigh against mine as we slowly moved around the dance floor. I patted my shirt pocket to make sure that I still had her number. Warning signals flashed in my head but I chose to ignore them. All the usual tell-tale signs were there but like a dumb stoned greenhorn in a stolen car, I thought I could beat that train to the crossing. Well, live and learn. Or maybe live, learn nothing and die. As it turned out, I learned a lot and a lot of people did die. But now all I wanted was to crawl into my bed and sleep for at least a year and a half. I had no open cases. I could sleep without worrying about keeping any appointments. The rent was paid. I had a few bucks in the bank. I was on easy street. I figured that I could just pass out and safely dream about Myra's rosebush. And dream I did.

THREE

And what dreams I had. I would probably
need Sigmund to decipher the strange shit
that bubbled up in my head when I slept.
Sometimes I remembered stuff but mostly I
didn't. What I did was wake up to the sound
of rain. A dim light made its way through my
yellowed shades. I checked the clock. It said
4:28 in the PM. I lay there trying to recall my
dreams. Sometimes I awoke with feelings of
elation and other times I woke up in a cold
sweat. These bad dreams left me feeling like
Frankenstein with the howling torch-bearing
villagers chasing me off a cliff. Ever since I
was a kid I had bad dreams. Maybe it was all
those meals of kielbasa and fried okra. My
father loved all that Polish crap but my
mother usually made soul food. He tried to
teach her to cook Polish but it never took to
his satisfaction. Nothing like knock down
drag out's at dinner. I threw up a lot. I still

felt guilty for wishing that they would both die so I could maybe, just maybe, eat a meal in peace. Now that they were gone I had all the peace I could ever hope for but, of course, it never satisfied. The past is never past and what ate at you back then still eats away today. The torture wheel of life just keeps on turning.

This is the wacky lunacy that still runs around in my head. I got out as soon as I could but those childhood traumas never go away. As a kid I was an outcast. Lucky for me I took my fathers coloring and could pass for a sort of swarthy Polack with kinky hair. But the truth always came out and that is when the shit hit the fan. But I did OK. I wasn't big but I was mean. My old man was a bastard but he taught me how to fight. More importantly he taught me when to fight, when to run, and how to make sure anybody that did screw with me never did it again. My mother was a good woman but why she took up with my father always left me scratching my head. He was an ignorant Polack garbage man. Not that she came from much either. Why they stuck it out as long as they did is beyond me. She eventually fell under the spell of Malcolm X and became a Black Muslim. She left the house one day and never came back. She got into some trouble with the government and had to take off for Algeria with some other newly minted Muslims. I never heard from her again. I have no idea if she is dead or alive. I think she was glad to see the end of both me and my now dead father. By that time I had had it anyway. I lied about my age and enlisted in the army.

I ended up doing duty as a clerk in the Panama Canal Zone. It was there that I picked up some Spanish, the clap, and a taste for Latin American food. To pass the time I took some courses in law enforcement thinking I could return to Chicago, become a cop, and enrich myself through graft and bribery. That didn't fly due to my Mother's status as a wanted fugitive. I wondered how they could let me in the Army but because of my mother, I couldn't be a cop. It sure left me with doubts about how the Feds did their background checks.

When I got out of the Army I got hired by a local agency as an investigator and that, along with some well placed greasing of the palms, led to a P.I. license. Most of what I did was legit but there were always ways to pick up extra change by doing favors for certain people. I took chances, chances that could have easily cost me my license but I didn't care. Staying straight or crossing over to the dark side made little difference to me. I was no Sam Spade. I had no code of honor. I liked what those hippies said. If it feels good then do it. That was the mantra of the day. I figured you only go around once. I lived for the moment and damn the torpedos. So far I had stayed out of jail and in one piece.

I dropped out of bed. I stretched. I did some deep knee bends. I could feel my blood start to flow once again. I took a quick shower. I started the coffee and made some toast. I called my message service. No job offers but I did get a message from one of my shady pals. Bats Locasio and I had hooked up way back in grade school. We pulled some stuff back in the day. I occasionally joined him in questionable endeavors if the profits sounded right. He was also a useful guy for some of the surveillance stuff I did whenever I got a legit client. He wanted me to meet him at Carmen's at seven. I had a few hours to kill. I cranked up the stereo. The Australian Jazz Quintet serenaded me as I did some housework. Usually I just let things go until I could bring a babe over. They were always appalled at the condition of my place and for whatever reason cleaned the place up. Well, the nice middle-class babes did. The pill poppers, dope heads, and junkies could care less about dust and a sink full of encrusted dishes. Sadly things had been a little slow in the chick department so I was forced to clean the place myself. I thought again of Myra. She did not strike me as a woman who would do any cleaning. I wondered just what she did for cash. She also was not like most women. They usually want to establish, right off the bat, an income base line. Myra didn't seem to be interested in what I did for a living or if I was broke or if I was flush. As a matter of fact she didn't ask one damn question. Maybe she wasn't interested. Maybe I was just a shield to escape the cops from hassling her that night. I thought I would give it a couple of days and then call her. I thought about Linko's warning. Maybe she was mobbed up. Maybe Bats knew who she was. Although he was certainly not likely to be running with any crowd she would be involved with. But everybody came from somewhere. Could be their paths had crossed somewhere along the line. Bats got around. I had never really met an Indian let alone one that was also black. Whatever her back story was, it had to be pretty damn interesting. As screwed up as my house was growing up, I could not imagine what hers was like. Did she live on a reservation? In the ghetto? In my line of work you get to meet all kinds. I learned early on that all people lie. They lie even when they don't have to. But they do anyway. Of course, I don't usually end up investigating righteous citizens. My clientele always have something to hide. Even the one's that hire me lie their heads off. It is never straight forward. I usually start out in a maze that I have to find my way out of. Clients, perps, cheats, and just plain assholes are the kind of people who inhabit my world. If I was a cynic when it came to people when I was a kid, I was now way beyond cynicism. That most people were scum was now a given. When you went in thinking that everyone was a liar and a selfish prick, then things could only go up from there. Even people who I sort of trusted never were given a pass. I played it as it lay. I figured I had to have my own back because no one else did.

I put the dust cloths away. I stowed the vacuum. I looked around with pride at the job I had done. At least the army had taught me how to straighten away my area in an emergency. I got dressed and headed out for some Italian at Carmen's nearby restaurant.

FOUR

As I passed through the revolving glass door the wonderful smell of tomato and garlic smacked me in the kisser. I was immediately transported to some Italian mother's kitchen. Carmen, with all his Sicilian gusto, greeted me with a hug.

"Welcome, Thorny. It is good to see you. Your shady pal is seated in the back. I keep telling you that you need to get rid of these street bandits and settle down. Find a nice girl and quit all this pazzo nonsense."

"Carmen, I'm glad you have my best interests at heart but right now my best interest is in some of the veal parm you cook so well. I have to join the street scum for business reasons. What can I say?"

We both laughed. He slapped me on the back, pinched my cheek, and pointed down the aisle to where Bats was sitting. He was a short and stocky guy. He had a pug nose, small mouth but big dark Italian eyes. His jet black hair was oiled and greased into a nice pompadour. He was wearing a green nylon shirt covered by a green Vegas gamblers jacket. Not hard to figure out where Bats had been these past few months. He spotted me and waved me forward. When I arrived he jumped up and shook my hand.

"Thorny, my man. It is good to see you, Been a while. I had to head out of town for a few months. Got too hot, if you catch my drift. Good to be back in goombah heaven. My mother could cook but not like Carmen."

"I heard on the jungle telegraph that there was some blowback on a blackmail scheme targeting a certain state bigwig. I smelled Bats all over that baby."

Bats grinned. "You get good reception on them airwaves you listen to. But better you don't know anymore than that. Anyway it is all copasetic now. No harm, no foul. A silly little misunderstanding between a certain high school cheer-leader slash baby-sitter that got resolved to all the parties satisfaction. I just had to go away for a spell, if you know what I mean. The heat is off me for now. But that is history. Onward and upward."

Carmen came by. Bats deferred to me. There was nothing that Carmen served up that was less than delicious.

"Two Ceasars, two veal parm's, and a little pasta. And bring us a bottle of that nice Italian red. Thanks, Carmen."

We ate and gossiped about who was in, who was out, and who was on the make. We talked jazz, blues, and Rock and Roll.

"When I was in Vegas laying low I saw Louis Prima and Keely Smith," bragged Bats. "They still got it. What a showman."

"Yeah, he is great. Whose pocket is he in? Never mind; I don't want to know. I caught Miles and Coltrane last month. Some show even if Miles spit at us and played with his back turned. No matter because the guy is a genius. Also caught Mel Torme; what a voice. How about we hit the Green Mill later?"

I told Bats about my meeting with Myra. He did not know her but he had heard that Lemmy the Shark, a local mob boss, was supposedly sporting some half breed chick around town. I wondered if that is who Myra was working for. Maybe I could pump Linko for more info. Or I could just ask her but I had the feeling that getting anything out of her would be a tricky proposition. I knew she had something going but just what it was would have to remain a mystery for now.

Bats and I finished up our meal. We had some grappa for the dinner's finale. We then got down to the business of why he had called me. Bats was an old pal but he never did anything unless there was money to be made.

"So here is the deal," he said. He leaned forward and whispered as if he were imparting state secrets.

"I get a call from a connection. You don't know this party. Seems a guy got a company. The said company distributes records, videos, cassettes, and shit like that. Seems stuff is disappearing. So he reaches out to my guy who reaches out to me. So I'm reachin' out to you."

"Wait a sec. Why don't this party just go to the cops?"

"Why do you think? Would you want the fuckin' cops playing in your sandbox?

Even if this guy was all legit the blue boys would want a handout just for showing up. You know how it works in this town. Nobody can just do their job. They gotta' have a little incentive. They gotta' get their hooks into you. And once in, it is hell to get out. Everybody is working everybody. You try to play it straight here and you are going to get screwed six ways to Sunday and never even get a kiss."

Bats mouth twisted up with distaste as he imparted his views on the business scene in Chicago. I found this more than a little entertaining considering he was part of the rot that ran through every transaction that took place in the city.

"I know but I had to ask. So what does this guy want?"

"He wants me to track down whoever is ripping him off."

"And when you find the party or parties, then what?"

"Never mind that. All I want is for you to help me nab the mooks doin' the deed. I figure maybe you go to work there and see what's what. I can't do it. I spent some time at this place and my face is now known. Should be a nice pay day when we finish up."

"Oh yeah? First off how much and secondly, do I become an accessory to murder when we catch up to these guys?"

Bats threw up his hands. "Murder? Who the hell is talking about murder?"

Bats had raised his voice and we were getting some strange looks from the other diners. I hushed Bats up.

"Easy, dude. These are things I have to know. I assume you are not going to turn these bad boys over to the cops so it is not out of the realm of possibility that this person or persons may find themselves weighed down by lead slugs and swimming with the fishes. But let us table that little question for now. Give me a number."

Bats heaved a heavy sigh. "Five G's."

"Five for me or the job?"

"The job. We split half and half."

"No way. I want at least four grand. Got to be half up front and half at the back end."

"Jesus, then I ends up with a measly grand. No thanks. I figured I was doing you a favor. I know the P.I. biz ain't doing shit so I come to you out of friendship. You know, to help out a pal."

"Sure, fine. I'll take three but that is it. Tell this guy you need more dough for your end. Let him know that certain people might be interested in his operation. Is he paying anybody off now?"

"I figure he has to be but if it ain't Lemmy the Shark then I don't know who. Maybe you can find out from this redskin you met. If she's the one Lemmy is banging then maybe you can charm her into feeding you some info. That is if Lemmy don't find out and have you done away with."

"Let me tell you, Bats. This dame ain't going to be charmed by anyone let alone me. Plus I doubt that she would be screwing a fat slob like Lemmy. You ever get a load of her and you would see why. This is no gun moll bimbo. But let me work on it. I got to call her. She gave me her number. Give me the weekend to see what I can find out. I'll call you on Monday and we can see this guy. If he pops for the upfront cash then I'll get on the job. Shouldn't be hard to spot who is doing the rip off. So, you up for a little jazz?"

"Why not. Who is playing tonight?"

"I think Gene Ammons and Sonny Stitt are in town."

"Now you're talkin'. Listen I know I asked you out here but after Vegas I'm a little light. I got a little carried away at the black jack table. Can you pick it up?"

"I figured you would pull this shit. You are a cheap bastard. I don't know why I have anything to do with you."

"Come on, Thorny. Who loves ya', baby. I brung you this gig, didn't I. I'll make it good. And maybe you can lay a C-note on me until we get some moolah from the company prez."

"Sure, why not? Want me to do your laundry and shine your shoes while I'm at it? By the way, who is this guy and what is the name of the company? I'll see what I can find out about his operation."

"No need. My guy says it's all kosher."

"Sure it is. And that is why the guy don't want no cops involved. Come on, Bats; spill."

"Just between me and you his name is Lester Jenkins. Company is Royal

Distribution. You happy now? Now come on so we can catch the first set. I got my dancin' shoes on. Maybe some of them sweet little working girls will be there."

"Didn't you get your fill of working girls in Vegas?"

"Jeez Thorny, I don't mean that. I mean those dolls what work at the bank and like Woolworth's. You know them lonely single girls that ain't no beauties but still got the right equipment to get the job done. What more could a babe like that want than a good looking hot Latin lover like me."

I had to smile at Bats. He was something else. I paid the bill, thanked Carmen, and handed Bats his C note. We headed south to the Green Mill and a night of jazz. I just hoped I wasn't stepping into some deep shit but I figured I owed Bats some leeway. A few years ago he helped me out with a situation that could have left me six feet under. Instead two guys were now at the bottom of Lake Michigan courtesy of Bats Locasio. It is hard to say no to someone who saved your life.

FIVE

"I'm waiting," she said answering the phone with an irritated voice.

"That is a hell of a way to say hello," I said. "This is Thorny."

"Thorny? What the hell is a thorny?"

"Come on, doll. How could you forget a handsome devil like me so soon? Behind the Uptown the other night? Cops after you? Dancing at Linko's?"

"Oh yeah. Now I got it. I did give you my number, didn't I?"

"Yes, you did. How about you pick me up in that hot little auto you got? I figured maybe a nice weekend up in Door County. Hike in the woods, swim in the lake. Maybe practice your tracking skills. Take a few scalps, steal some horses. How does that sound?"

"It sounds like you are as goofy as your name. I'll ignore the racist attempts at humor. I have engagements that can't be avoided. How about instead we try this. You want to feel the road-hugging moves that my little Bavaria can make then how about a quick buzz up to Milwaukee? I've got a taste for the goodies at Frenchie's. Have you eaten there?"

"Milwaukee? Are you kidding? What's wrong with Chicago? Why go up there with all those Polacks?"

"Wait a minute. Didn't you tell me you were Polish?"

"Oh, so now you remember me. Yes, I did. There are enough Polacks here. I don't need to travel to another state to find more. You ever have Polish food? How about we go for a spin and then I'll take you to the White Eagle."

"I don't like Polish food. It is way too heavy. I have to maintain my figure. It takes skill and strength to hunt down buffalo on horseback."

"OK, you win. Do I need to dress?"

"I hope so. They don't serve naked people even in a hick town like Milwaukee."

"I mean suit and tie?"

"At least. Where do I find you? It has got to be tomorrow night. After that I'm busy."

I gave her the particulars. We set a time. Now I was hot to see her despite her pretending to not remember me. I wondered if she knew that I was a P.I. I had a sneaking suspicion that she was working me. I did not know why I felt this way. Maybe Linko had told her about me. Not that he knew much beyond the fact that I was a P.I. who worked on both sides of the line. As hot as I was for her I knew better than to trust anyone. She hardly struck me as someone who would be shagging a pig like Lemmy the Shark but you never know. I would have to move slowly. Let her show her hand first. Maybe she was after something. I knew what I was after. Maybe she would send out smoke signals that I could read. As long as I didn't get scalped.

I smacked myself in the head. I was thinking like a moron with all this Indian shit. She was probably as much an Indian as I was a Polish sausage maker. I had never known an Indian. I began to wonder what they were like. It was sort of like the Chinese or

Philipinos that I knew lived in the city but what the hell did I know about them? Nothing is what I knew. All I knew about Indians came from the movies. Redskins chasing John Wayne in Stagecoach. Tonto and Scout. That was about it. I did see some of them hanging out in front of the two Indian bars in Uptown. Sometimes they would be passed out in the street until the cops picked them up. There was also an Indian Center just south of the Green Mill. I wondered what went on in there but I never bothered to go inside. Chicago had every ethnic group but the whites stayed together. The black people also stayed in their own area like the Chinese and the Mexicans. It was as if we all lived in separate countries. Going to grade school and high school everyone was white. One time a kid from Alabama showed up in my junior year and he was fawned over as some exotic creature. All the girls went ga-ga for his accent. I wonder what we would have made of a colored person or an Indian? Now I was really juiced to see this Myra dame. I decided to go to the Library the next day and look up Crow Indians. I could dazzle her with my knowledge of her people. Or maybe she knew nothing herself. Maybe she never knew her mother or father. Maybe she was the product of a hooker hook-up. I was really ignorant on the subject. Were Indian girls even working as hookers? And who could her father be? Maybe she made the whole thing up. Maybe she wasn't either black or Indian. I looked in the mirror. I told myself to knock it off. I was beginning to think like a white person. After all, what the hell was I? I felt much more white than black. I had been confused all my life. I had never really felt as comfortable with blacks as I did with whites. Maybe seeing her was a big mistake. I was confused enough. Or maybe I was thinking about this all wrong. This was too much thinking and all I did was twist myself up in knots with questions that I could not answer.

I was sitting in my kitchen. My hand was soaking in hot water. I had hurt it punching that mook outside The Green Mill. Bats had gotten up to his usual shit. I should have never taken him to the place. He was fine for the first set. But after three drinks he was getting feisty. He went over to a table with three couples and asked one of the ladies to dance. Her husband told him to fuck off. A big mistake. I was a regular at the club and did not want to get 86'd. I got up from our table

"Bats, how about we head out. Don't ruin these peoples night."

"I ain't ruining nobodies night. All I did was ask the dame for a dance," babbled Bats.

"Well, maybe she don't want to dance."

The guy, a big guy, who had told Bats to leave, started to get up. I pushed him back down.

"Look pal, leave it. You don't want to get into it with Bats here. He didn't mean anything. I'll take care of him."

The guy looked up at me. He wasn't sure what to do. I had seen Bats in action. I didn't want to see it in here.

"Hey, dick head," Bats said. "How about we see if the little lady here wants to dance. How about it, honey. Care to shake it with me?"

The guy got up and reached for Bats. That is when I clipped him. He sat back down in his chair. I looked at the rest of the table. No one looked eager to start anything. I grabbed Bats and pushed him outside.

"What the hell is wrong with you? Why do you always start trouble?"

"Trouble? I asked the dame to dance."

"She is with that guy. Pick on a single dame, one that ain't with someone. Jesus, now my hand is killing me. Come on, I'm putting you in a cab. Go home and I'll call you on Monday."

"OK, sure Thorny. I guess I am a little beat."

I shoved Bats into a cab and gave the driver Bat's address. I went back into the club. I apologized to the guy I hit. He wasn't up for anymore. They were probably stock brokers or something out slumming and looking for a little excitement but not this much excitement. I bought them a round of drinks. I apologized to the owner of the place. He said it was no problem but he didn't want to see Bats in the place again. There had been incidents in the past. Bats was a good guy to have your back in a scrap but him and alcohol did not match up so good. I began to have my doubts about this deal he had dragged me into. I would have to wait and talk to this shipping guy and see for myself if this was legit or if Bats was enlisting me in something even hinkier than what he said it was.

It was time for a Scotch on the rocks and a little late night Dave Brubeck. I liked to sip and listen while I looked out my front window at the rising moon. In short order, despite my aching hand, I nodded out while Dave pounded away on Balcony Rock.

SIX

I had on my one and only summer weight suit. I had a striped tie around my neck and freshly shined ox blood loafers on my feet. I had those tootsie's encased in silk socks. I checked myself out in the mirror and nodded my approval. I had just stepped out side. Before I could even take a deep breath, she pulled up in a cloud of dust. Hiawatha with hot wheels. I opened the passenger side door and crawled in. She smelled as good as she looked. It was that scent again. She smiled. I smiled. As soon as I shut the door she peeled away from the curb.

"You look great," I said.

"Yes, I do. You doll up OK yourself. So tell me, Thorny. What's your deal? I know you are a P.I. who is not averse to playing ball with both sides of the law. The jungle grapevine, I'm happy to say, gives you a thumbs up."

"I figured you would pump Linko for info. Who else on the grapevine do you know? Who you working for?"

She laughed. She flashed a mouthful of big white teeth. She turned to me at a traffic light. Seeing her in the daylight showed me her almost copper-toned complexion. The combination of black and Indian blood, if that is what she was, gave her face a bold beauty that took my breath away. She was a stunning woman. Her dark eyes flashed. My heart skipped a beat.

"Let's not talk shop now. Come on, this is a first date. Let's talk jazz or movies or something. Let's keep it light until we see where this night leads. I got a pretty good idea where you want it to lead. I just need a little more time with you."

"Myra, I promise to be a gentleman until indications point me in another direction."

She laughed out loud. This caused her ample bosom to bounce lightly. I think I fell hard for her right then and there. It was at that point that we hit the expressway. Myra may have never heard of Stirling Moss but she drove like him. She handled that BMW like a pro with a three lap lead at the Indy 500. She was wearing a blue and white summer dress. Her long black hair had a shine that glowed. On her feet she had soft-soled driving shoes and on her hands were lamb skin gloves. She worked that 5 speed gearbox like it was part of her. I was smiling all the way to the Milwaukee lake front. She pulled up in front of Frenchie's. Before turning the car over to the valet she removed her gloves. She reached behind us and came up with a pair of white pumps. She slipped out of her driving shoes and put on the heels. She retrieved a small white purse. She handed the valet her keys.

"Be careful with my baby or you will wish you had never seen me. Do you understand?"

The man was staring at her with his mouth open. He nodded.

"I will treat her like my most precious possession. Don't you worry, lady."

We entered the fancy French restaurant. It looked like some Hollywood version of a French whore house. Thick carpet, red flocked walls and a staff right out of central casting.

"Ah, It is good to see, Madame" said the host with a phony French accent. He had a big moustache and slicked back hair. "I have your favorite table ready."

I was to soon learn that Myra was no squaw off the rez. She knew her way around classy joints like this in a way I had yet to learn.

A fawning man with an armful of menu's led us to a table near the front of the place. It was where everyone entering would have to pass us. We were seated at a table adorned with white damask linen and a large array of cutlery and glassware. I let out a low whistle.

"This is some fancy joint," I said.

"I hope I am not putting you out of your league, Thorny," she said. "Let me know if you need any help with the French menu. Probably some of the items will be unfamiliar to you."

I smiled and stayed quiet. A waiter approached our table. He bowed. She ordered. We ate. We sipped wine and talked jazz. Our tastes seemed to slide along on the same rail. Miles, Duke, Coltrane, Chet, Bill Evans. I was partial to Ella but she was into

June Christy. We finished off a great meal with Crepes Suzette and French Press coffee. I was feeling no pain. I was no longer trying to figure out her angle. I was smitten. Her dark hair and eyes glowed like a lighthouse beacon beckoning a lost sailor. Her large features highlighted by high cheek bones and her generous red-lipped mouth mesmerized me like a snake charmer wooing a python. I wanted to climb across the table and take her right there. A fire was ignited in my loins to such an extent that I wondered if I would be able to stand up without embarrassing us both. And yet I had the feeling that this woman did not get embarrassed easily.

She excused herself to visit the powder room. I called over the waiter and paid the exorbitant bill. It was worth every penny just to be able to sit across from Myra. All I could think of is how she had felt in my arms at the after hours club. I wanted her naked and beneath me. Or on top of me; I didn't care as long as we were together. I hadn't felt like this about a dame since high school when one of the school cheer leaders, a blond goddess, let me play stink finger behind the school sports field. She was out for cheap thrills with the colored kid and I was just ga-ga. She laughed while I shot a wad into my BVD's. I was so hot now that if Myra so much as blew in my ear then I would have another load in my pants.

The drive back to my place flashed by in a daze. She drove like a professional wheelman. I asked her if this is what she did. She laughed and did not answer. She pulled up in front of my apartment building. I looked over at her.

"How about you come up and we put an exclamation point to this beautiful evening."

"Why Thorny, this is our first date. What kind of girl do you think I am? You buy me a dinner and then I have to give it up? Sorry buddy but it does not work like that. At least not with me. I don't know what kind of bimbo's you usually run with but I am not one of them."

I lost control. I grabbed her by the shoulder and tried to pull her close for a kiss. She swung a left cross that caught me on the side of my head. My noggin bounced off the car window. I saw stars. She got out of the car. She came around to my side. She opened the door and pulled me out of the car. I stood, weak kneed and holding my head.

"See what happens to fresh boys? I like you Thorny but you have to behave. I am no wide-eyed kid that you wine and dine then bang and toss away. You go upstairs and work off that lust. Call me when you are ready to act like an adult and not a hot and bothered teenager."

I stood there under the streetlight staring at her like I was the village idiot. She had slugged me. I never saw that coming. I stood mute, holding my head. Before I could say anything she pulled me close to her. Her perfume filled my brain. Her strong hands held me by my shoulders. She leaned in close to me. I could feel her hot sweet breath on my cheek.

"Listen to me. Do not, I repeat, do not do this thing with Bats Locasio. Find a way out of it. Don't ask me any questions. Go away. Lay low. Don't call me again. Leave a message with Gimpy at the pool hall. You know who he is, the place by the

Riviera Theater. Tell him where you are and I'll get in touch."

"You mean that old guy at that pool hall by Linko's place?"

Without a further word she pushed me away from her. She got in her speed box and roared off into the night. I stood transfixed. Between the punch and the warning I was all at sea. What the hell was going on? Just who was this dark beauty? How the hell did she know about Bats and the deal he had enlisted me in? What did that guy from the pool hall have to do with this? I stood in the humid air of the hot Chicago night and watched her red tail lights fade away. I was rarely at a loss for words but this time I was speechless. But even if I could talk who could I talk to? There was obviously more going on than just a simple investigation into some stolen Sinatra sides. I broke out in a cold sweat. Maybe I had been playing just a little too fast and loose with the line between the good guys and the bad guys. Now I was worried. I had to make a decision.

SEVEN

Lionel Hampton was playing softly. I sat staring out my window. It was a humid night. The yellow streetlights cast a soft glow on the quiet area in front of my building. I was sipping my third Dewers on the rocks. My mind was reeling. I was at a loss as to just what I should do. How in hell did Myra know about Bats? He had told me that he did not know her. Was Bats setting me up? He had always been straight with me in the past. Was he in deep shit with someone? Was I being made the fall guy for some scene I knew nothing about? If she had info on something going down then why not just lay it out for me? How deep into this stuff was she?

I had my .38 by my side. I was nervous. I made a decision. I dialed Bats number. It rang for a long time.

"Who is this?" said a sleepy female voice.

"I need to talk to Bats."

"Bats ain't here. Who is this?"

"A business associate. Do you know where he is?"

"No I don't. You know what time it is?"

"Never mind that. Are you going to see him?"

"I hope so seeing as he lives here."

It suddenly sank in that I never knew who Bats lived with or if he had a steady dame. Was this dame a wife? A some time squeeze? His mother? It hit me hard that even though Bats had saved my life once I was really never interested in learning more about him. This was basic P.I. training and I had dropped the ball.

"Listen because this is important. You tell him that Thorny had to leave town on a job. Tell him I won't be able to see him on Monday. Tell him I'll be in touch. You got that? It is important."

"Hold on, I got to write this down. He never said anything about a Thorny. You in the shipping business with him?"

Shipping business? What the hell was she talking about? And just who was she?

"Just write it down. Thorny can't make it on Monday. That's all. Tell him that. Sorry to wake you up, Mrs. Locasio. You are the Mrs, ain't you?"

"Just who else would I be? Is this shit legit? What the hell is he up to now? I don't like the sound of this phone call."

"Relax. Just pass on the message. It's business. No need to worry."

I hung up the phone before she could ask me anything else. Now I was even more worried then before. I threw some things in a suitcase. I took two boxes of ammo and my sawed-off 12 gauge. I put on my shoulder holster. I checked my .38 for the tenth time. I spun the cylinders. All the chambers were loaded with hollow points. I filled up a thermos with coffee. I grabbed a box of stale doughnuts that had adorned my crusty counter for the last week.

I went down the back stairs. I opened the door to the parking area with caution. I didn't see anyone. I hurried to my rusty Chevy. I threw my case in the back seat. I got in and started the clunker up. I pulled out and headed north. I figured to lay low in Highwood until I could find out what was going on. An old family friend, Stippy Kowalski, had a small restaurant and club up there. He had a coach house behind the joint that was my home for a while when I got out of the service. I mustered out of the army at Fort Sheridan which adjoined Highwood where Stippy's joint was located. After I got out of the army I stayed in the place for a few months. Stippy was a stand-up guy who asked no questions. His wife, Berta, was a magician in the kitchen. I could already taste her Polish specialties.

Sheridan Road was deserted at this time of night. I drove slowly. My mind was reeling. Was I doing the right thing in heeding Myra's warning? Why should I trust her over Bats? Was I thinking with my head or my dick? Bats I knew from childhood. But after speaking to that woman on the phone I wondered just how well I knew him. Myra was almost a stranger. But there was something in her voice that gave me the jitters. She knew something. Too late to second guess myself now.

Jesus, me and dames. It was never just normal man and woman stuff. It was always high drama, heartbreak, demented entanglements. I sure knew how to pick them. Or maybe it was just the luck of the draw. No, it was me. And here I was once again knee deep in who knows what. Well, so far no laws had been broken. Bats could always find another fool to do whatever was needed for this caper.

I pulled into the driveway alongside Stippy's house which adjoined the restaurant. The place was closed up. I didn't want to disturb Stippy or Berta. I had a key to the place. They would see my car in the morning. I got my stuff out of the back seat. I climbed the stairs to the coach house. I put the key in the lock and opened the door. I probably should have made sure that no one else was staying there. As I opened the door it occurred to me how careless I was becoming. For all I knew someone with a shotgun just like mine could be staying in the coach house and I could easily be mistaken for a burglar and get my head shot off. I was lucky; the place was empty. Nothing much had changed since I was last here. There was a sofa bed, a table and chairs, and a broken TV. A small closet and bathroom sat at the back. I dropped my stuff on the floor. Suddenly I was exhausted. I lay on the couch without opening the bed. I fell asleep. I had dreams and nightmares but I did not remember any of them when I was woken in the morning. Stippy was shaking me as I pried my crusty eyes open. I stared into his smiling face.

"Thorny! What the hell are you doing here? Why didn't you call and say you were coming. If you had arrived a few days ago you would have scared the shit out of Berta's cousin who was visiting us. Are you in some kind of trouble?"

I rubbed the remaining sleep from my eyes. Outside I could see a steady rain coming down. I swung my legs off the couch. I stood up and hugged Stippy.

"Something like that. The less you know the better off you'll be. I just need to lay low for a few days. I'll pay whatever the going rate is."

"Never mind that. I got your back. You look skinny. Hang around a while and Berta will fatten you up. I'll tell her you're here. I'll make sure she keeps it a secret. Just tell me what you need."

"You're the best, Stippy. I just got to figure a few things out. Is the phone on up here?"

"Sure it is. Do what you need to do. I'll have Berta fix you up some breakfast or you want to come down to the house?"

"No, I better stay out of sight. This town has some eyes and ears and I don't want anyone to spot me. Here are my car keys. Can you pull it into the garage and throw a tarp over it?"

"You got it, Thorny. I'll be back in a few minutes."

I sat back down. I was exhausted despite sleeping for hours. I rubbed my bloodshot eyes and tried to concentrate. Who could I call to get a line on this shit that was coming down? Should I even try and call anyone? If Myra knew something then why didn't she tell me straight up? Should I call her? Maybe her line was tapped. Could the Feds be in on this? But why would they be interested in some small time truck heist? My contacts with the Chicago P.D. had shorted out a long time ago. Whatever favors I was owed were long ago used up. I was flying solo. I decided to put off everything until I had some coffee. Berta was probably fixing me up some eggs and kielbasa right now. She had been like a second mother to me when I left the army. It was good to know that such kind-hearted people still inhabited this jungle. Living in the midst of Chicago's corrupt world tended to make a guy forget that such a thing as simple goodness was still out there. There was no hidden agenda with Stippy and Berta. I just hoped that my hiding out here did not bring down any evil on their heads.

EIGHT

Berta fed me, kissed me, and left to get things going in the restaurant.

"So explain to me again about this Indian woman," said Stippy. "Give me a description. I still got people in the city. Let me see what I can find out."

"It sure is strange. I mean she seemed fine. I had seen her around Linko's, you know, that after hours joint. But the strange thing was that when I found her in the parking lot she had on a wig. I guess a lot of alarm bells should have gone off. I mean why would she need to be going around in a disguise? And I really should have known something was not kosher when that fat fuck Linko seemed to know her and also seemed to be watching out for her."

"I guess you should have realized a lot of things, Thorny. But I know how it is. The dick gets hard and the brain gets soft. But none of this makes any sense. Just think about it. How would she know about your deal with Bats? And what are you doing with that madman anyway? He is nothing but trouble. You keep screwing around with these criminals and you know where you'll end up."

"I know, Stippy. But Bats, we go way back and he saved my ass once when I was about to buy it."

"I get it but he is nothing but a one way ticket to the joint or the morgue. It's a miracle he's still above ground. And why should she warn you off? What's her play? What's her angle? You're right I don't get it. I'll put out some feelers. Meanwhile we have Billy Little and his band coming in tonight. Have you heard him? They are terrific. He goes from Desmond to Coltrane in the same tune. You can sit upstairs with Berta where no one will see you. Now I have to run. I got lots to get ready for tonight's show. I'll get you some food later."

"Thanks Stippy. I'm going to crash and give my head a rest. If you hear anything, let me know."

I made my way back to the couch. I opened it into a full size bed. My head was spinning. I was totally confused. Would Bats sell me out? And sell me out to who? Did he even know what was going on? Was I losing my edge? All I had were questions and nowhere to find any answers. I sat on the edge of the bed. I stared out the back window of the coach house. The trees were in full leaf. The rain had let up. The full branches swayed in the hot damp breeze. Lake Michigan was just a short ways off. Highwood bordered on Fort Sheridan. It was a military base used as a meeting place for the Illinois National Guard. It was also a recruiting site for the 5th Army. I had spent time there when I had mustered out of the army. While I was there all I did was play golf and use the available boats to go fishing. If only the taxpayers knew how their taxes were being pissed away on places like this. Who am I kidding? Waste is what the government, be it national or local, does best. But that was not my problem. I needed answers and I needed them now. I got out my phone book and looked up a number. Maybe that guy from the pool hall could help me. We had never really spoken but he was good enough to wave me off on that night I went to see him. He must have done that for a reason. I dialed the number hoping he would remember me.

"Your dime; start talking."

"Is this the pool hall above the Riviera?"

"It was last time I looked. Who wants to know?"

"Listen, I don't know if you remember me. This is Thorny Pilsudski. You recall that time I came up there to see you and you waved me off for some reason? I'm calling because Myra Rosebush told me to use you to let her know where I am."

There was a pause. All I could hear was shouting and the clacking of cue balls.

"Give me a number and I'll pass it on."

I gave him the number on the black phone that was on the table next to the now opened couch. He hung up before I could ask anything else. I waited. I tried to think of who else I might call in order to get some information. I drew a blank. The cops were out of reach. They all hated P.I.'s anyway. I was going to go crazy waiting for her to get back to me. How the hell did I ever get in this mess? Maybe I was making a mountain out of a mole hill. It could be that she heard something and was jumping to conclusions. But again I wondered why the mystery? Nothing made any sense. I was beginning to feel like some poor sap character out of a cheap pulp crime novel. You know; the poor schmuck who gets suckered in by a dame with a hidden agenda. Is that what this was? I really wanted to get hold of Bats and find out just what the story was but something kept holding me back. Sure, Bats had once saved my bacon but I still never really trusted him. Would he have my back or just step over me? It's bad when someone holds a marker on your soul.

To pass the time I tried to work out a little. I did jumping jacks, push-ups, and sit-ups. I kept it up until I broke a sweat. I cleaned and oiled my weapons. I called my message service but there had been no requests for my services. This wasn't unusual. Most of my work came from previous client referrals. I had been on my last job for a long time. It had involved following a suspect all over the states. It was a convoluted corporate fraud case. I delivered my reports but I never did learn the outcome. A lot of times big corporations cover up any malfeasance to avoid bad publicity for the firm in question. That is the way things worked. The richer and more powerful you were, the better your chances of avoiding the law. The big boys, any of the big boys, rarely paid the price for their misdeeds. So, call it flawed logic or whatever you want, but this is why I never had any hang-ups about doing things that were not strictly legit. A straight arrow in this town meant a one-way ticket to loserville. Look at the way the religious leaders carried on. The Cardinal lived like a prince. Jesse Jackson was always walking around in custom made leather suits followed by a squad of body guards. If I tried to run a backroom card game I would either be busted or would have to pay off to the cops in a big way. But the churches regularly held Las Vegas style gambling nights. They didn't pay off in either bribes or taxes. The only saving grace of a system like this is that there was no ambiguity. You knew what was what from the get go. You want to play then you got to pay. I played, sometimes I paid, and sometimes I got paid. The scale was never balanced. You had to grab what you could while the blind lady held her scales and hope for the best.

NINE

I had just started to doze off when the phone rang. I picked it up but said nothing. It was her.

"Thorny, you there?"

"What the hell is going on? Why did you tell me to get away from Bats? What is happening?"

"I'll fill you in later. Where are you? I have to see you."

I told her. There was a pause. I heard her breathing.

"Fine. I know the place. I've been there a few times to catch some acts. But listen carefully. I am not going to drive there. Too many people know my car. I'll take the train and grab a cab to the place. You won't recognize me. I'll find you."

"I'm in a coach house behind the club. If you get here later I'll be upstairs above the bandstand. Ask for Stiffy. He's the owner. Just how much trouble am I in?"

She had closed the phone. I sat and stared at the receiver in my hand. What the hell was all this? I was tempted to just drive home. All this cloak and dagger shit was getting on my nerves. I once again began to doubt my own motives. Why would I take her word over a guy who had literally saved my life? Was it just because I was hot for her or was it something else? I had survived this far by following my gut. Was this just more of the same thing. I wanted to hear her out. But mostly I wanted to see her again. The way she had felt in my arms when we danced came back to me with a rush of emotion. The way she moved and the way she smelled was so powerful that I could still feel her presence. Jesus, I was acting like a teen-ager. I began to feel ridiculous. I was always looking down at the poor saps that I followed around while snapping pics of their adulterous behavior. Maybe I was the sap now. Broads are a dime a dozen is what I had always said. What was it with this one? Sure, she was beautiful and had a bod and a half but so did a lot of other women. I couldn't put my finger on it. Maybe she was a bruja ; one of those Indian witches I had read about. Maybe she had put a spell on me. Now I was too nervous to sleep. I wanted the night to fall. I wanted a lot of things but whether or not I would get them was not up to me. I felt helpless. What the hell was happening to me?

I jumped up at the sound of someone knocking on the door. I had been so lost in my reveries that I had not heard anyone climbing the stairs. I grabbed the sawed-off shotgun and cocked both hammers. I approached the side of the door.

"What?" I said.

"It's me, Thorny. I got some dinner for you."

I peeked through the curtain. It was Stiffy. He was carrying a tray. I opened the door. I was assaulted by the smell of pork and hot sauerkraut. I suddenly realized just how hungry I was.

"Berta cooked for you. You go ahead and eat. Put down that damned gun. Just how much trouble are you in? Relax; you're safe here. I'll come and get you when the band starts. It'll be dark by then and we can go up the back way to the office over the stage. Have you heard anything from anyone?"

"She called. She's coming here later. She said she will be in disguise. I told her to ask for you. If she shows while I'm up with Berta then just send her up there. You hear anything from Chicago?"

"Gimme Steffelbach? You remember him? Does the odd job for Lemmy's outfit?"

"Yeah, I know who he is. A real lowlife scumbag."

"He is that, for sure, but he does me a favor now and then. It's a long story but anyway I go the back way around in getting the lowdown on this dame. Gimme is not for sure but he overhears some guys at the Amici Club, you know the one on Taylor Street where the goomba's hang out? Anyway these mooks are making talk about this new hit man in town. Seems that Lemmy imported new talent for some job and the talk is that the guy is not a guy but a dame. One guy says he seen her and she's a knockout. He didn't get anything else but maybe that's your dame."

"That is just nuts, Stippy. Even if it's true why would she be telling me anything? I don't get it. It sounds like Gimme is full of shit. I bet the little creep wanted a pay-off for the info. He probably made the whole thing up."

Stippy waved his hand in the air. I had started in on my supper. It was delicious. Berta was great with Polish food. I felt like a kid again at my mother's table.

"You are probably right," said Stippy. "Gimme is a dumb little shit but he is usually straight with me. Anyway, I guess you'll find out tonight. You enjoy the food and I'll be back later. I think there is a radio in the closet. You can catch the White Sox game. The TV as you can see is busted. See you later, Thorny."

"Sure thing. Thank Berta for the food."

Once Stippy left I continued eating. Could the info from Gimme be right? A female hit man? I never heard of such a thing. It was common for the mob to use out of town talent for hits but I never heard of a dame doing that kind of work. Jesus, could it be that she liked me and that Bats was the target? Was she going to off Bats? Christ but this shit was driving me crazy. I looked at the clock. I still had a few hours to wait. I finished eating. I found the radio in the closet. I plugged it in. I could care less about the White Sox but I had to do something to keep my mind from spinning. I lay back on the bed and listened to the Pale Hose blow another game. The last time the Sox were in the World Series the city had set off the air raid alarms and scared the shit out of the whole town. People ran to their basements in fear of Russian bombers. Heads rolled from that little screw-up. Only in Chicago. Despite my anxiety I managed to doze off.

TEN

Stippy came to get me. He was dressed in a brown suit with a fat red tie. All these years in America and he still looked like a Polack just off the boat.

"Stippy," I said. "You got to get some new threads. It looks like you are still wearing your communion suit."

"Never mind the ball busting. It is a good suit so I wear it. These new fashions ain't for a guy like me."

I laughed and patted him on the back He led me downstairs. We went up to the back of the club. I was now in the Green Room with the band. Introductions were made.

"How is it I ain't seen you guys play?" I asked.

Billy Little, the leader and sax player smiled. He had conked hair, light brown skin, and a big smile. "You got me, boss.

Maybe because we been playing back east for the last six months. You know; Baltimore, Philly, and D.C."

"Well I hear good things. You guys get a record deal yet?"

"I wish. Our manager says he is talking with Blue Note. I think he's full of shit. You got any clout?"

"Me, no. But I'll put the word out wherever I can."

"That's cool, my man. Hope you dig our sound."

"I'm sure I will. Stippy says he hears you guys are great."

"Well, I hope we get a nice crowd. We are hoping to get something steady in Chicago. I think we done had enough of the road for a while."

"Has your agent talked to the folks at the Green Mill? They always get a good crowd especially on the weekends."

"I sure hope so. Maurey does his best but I don't think he got the clout he says he does."

"Isn't he here tonight?" I asked.

The other guys in the band started laughing. Billy was smiling at me.

"Look, don't get me wrong. Maurey tries but I don't think we are going anywhere with him. He said he had family business to attend to but will show up later. We had to rent a van just to get our stuff up here. I had to front the cash. And he still owes us from the gigs back east."

"I can see where you guys are none to happy. You got a contract with this Maurey?"

"No, we never signed anything. He keeps asking but I ain't that dumb. We said first we see what he can do for us. I mean he got us the gigs back east but the pay was for shit and we ain't seen half of it. Some of the guys got families."

I turned to Stippy. "Maybe you can help these guys out. You know agents in the city."

"Sure I do. I thought you gentlemen were well represented. Let me put out the word that the hottest jazz combo in town is looking for new representation and a record deal. If Blue Note shows any interest then the guys I know can work a much better deal than this Maurey character can probably negotiate."

Billy nodded. "Thanks, man. But as long as we are being on the up and up then how about you pay us up front."

Stippy did not look happy. "Listen Billy, you know that ain't how it works. I made a deal with your manager for a set price plus a piece of the take. He said he would be here later tonight, after the gig, to collect."

"Sure but see, as of now, he ain't no longer our manager or agent. You said you can do us better. You sign any contract for tonight with him?"

"No, it was all last minute over the phone. He called me and said you guys had an off night. I got to say he sold you guys cheap. I heard good things from Philly so I agreed."

Billy stood up. He did not look happy.

"And just what are we getting paid?"

"He said you do three sets tonight. $350 for the night."

"That cheap bastard. He told us we had to do this gig gratis for the exposure. Then he didn't show up at the van rental place. I got hold of him. He said to just pay the freight and he would pay us back. Wait until I get my hands on his scrawny ofay neck."

The four other guys in the group shouted a barrage of obscenities.

"So, like I said Mr. Kowalski. You want a group playing here tonight then you hand over that money or we walk. I'll take care of Maurey if and when he shows up later. We got a deal?"

Stippy looked at me. I shrugged my shoulders. It wasn't my money or my decision. If it was up to me I would give them the cash. I knew how much musicians were ripped off by agents, managers, and record companies. We had a perfect example right here in Chicago with Chess Records. The city had the best jazz and blues players in the country and they almost all worked for peanuts. They had to keep day jobs just to stay afloat. I guess Stippy felt the same way because he gave Billy the money.

People were starting to come over from the restaurant. I went out back and up another set of stairs to the office. Berta was sitting there at her desk working on the books. She smiled when I walked in.

"Thorny, it is so good to see you."

She got out of her chair and gave me a rib-crushing hug. Berta was gray-haired and stout. She had a big smile that lit up her wide Polish face along with the whole room. I kissed her on both cheeks.

"Berta, you spoil me. The dinner was great. Just like my mother used to make except you are a much better cook."

She waved her hand at me. "You are a good boy, Thorny. Come and sit. We can hear the show from here. You think these boys will bring in a crowd?"

"I hope so. They got good write-ups from back east."

"Stippy has not told me much but I know you are in trouble. I hope it is not anything serious."

"No, don't worry Berta. I am just not sure about a few things. Someone is coming here tonight and I hope everything will get straightened out. Don't you fret about it."

She patted my hand and went back to doing her figures. I stepped outside on the balcony and looked out over the club. The bandstand was bathed in a soft blue light. The sound system had been pumping out some Count Basie. Stippy shut it down and got up to give his spiel about upcoming events. He then introduced the Billy Little Quartet. Billy walked on stage and stepped up to the mike. He counted it down. The band started playing Stormy Weather. Billy stepped out front and started to solo. His first chorus sounded just like Ben Webster. He then segued into what would have an uncanny resemblance to the sound of Paul Desmond. He then blew the changes like Stan Getz. He did a chorus like Sonny Rollins and then finished off with a Coltrane blitz of notes. It was an astounding feat that had the crowd clapping in appreciation. He bowed. Thorny appreciated the feat that Billy had just pulled off but he was also a little offended by the slickness of it. He felt it was like a comedian who only did impressions. When the applause died down, Billy stepped up to the microphone.

"That was a bow to those who came before us. They set the sound for the tenor sax. Now I want to introduce my band and get into what we do."

He proceeded to introduce the other guys one by one. He had a piano, guitar, bass, and drums behind him. After some more enthusiastic applause they broke into a unique up tempo version of Night in Tunisia. They sounded tight. Billy showed his chops on a few other standards. They then went into original material. It was a stunning display of musicianship. Ollie, his guitar player reminded Thorny of Pat Martino. After 40 minutes the band left the stage leaving only Billy alone with his horn. He proceeded to do a solo version of My Foolish Heart. It was breath taking in its sweet melodic vibratoless long-held notes. Thorny was filled with emotion as each long note went straight to his heart. It was a stunning piece of playing. The audience rose to its feet with thunderous applause as the last note seeped out of Billy's horn.

The place had filled up. Berta was beside me surveying the crowd and smiling.

"I think these boys are good for business. But for me I like a good polka." She laughed out loud. I joined her. The music and the slivovitz that Berta had offered me had left me feeling no pain.

"So what did you think?"

I turned at the sound of Billy's voice.

"You guys sounded great," I said. "I had no idea that you could play like you just did. It was one of the most beautiful things I have ever heard. You have got to get recorded. I don't think you'll have any trouble finding gigs in the city. Also you got Milwaukee and Gary nearby. Plenty of work. Stippy has a lot of connections."

"I guess we do have some kind of a following. I spotted this woman in the crowd who came to see us back east. I had a couple of drinks with her in D.C. Thought I might get some. She is a fine lookin' lady but no luck. I went after her on the break but I can't find her. You spot her? Long blonde hair, all in black?"

My warning system went off. I went back to the balcony railing outside the office. I scanned the crowd. I didn't see her.

"Sounds good, Billy. I got to get something from my place. See you for the next set." I waved a goodbye to Berta.

I headed down the stairs and out the back. I ran up the long flight of steps to the coach house. I opened the door and there she was. She must have removed the blonde wig. Her black hair glistened under the floor lamp. She was dressed in a black jump suit and black boots. There was a large duffel bag at her feet. She got out of the chair and came up to me. I opened my mouth to speak. She put her hand over my lips. She shook her head. She motioned for me to take a seat. She went and shut the light. We were in shadows. The only light came from the full moon. Colored lights from the back of the club gave the single room an eerie glow. She took a seat across from me. I waited for an explanation. I got one but it sure was a hundred degrees away from what I expected to hear. Although the truth is I had no idea about what she was going to say.

She sighed and a heavy look came over her strong features. She had her hands clasped between her knees. She looked up at me. Her eyes seemed to hold an ocean of regret.

"I do free lance wet work. You know what that is, I assume."

I sat back in the chair that I was perched upon. I figured a lot of things that she might be into but this was not one of them. It took me a few beats before I could speak. I looked at her hard. For some reason

I found what she had said difficult to process. I knew what Gimme had told Stippy about the female hit man but I had dismissed it as Gimme's usual bull shit. I somehow didn't want to accept it. It upset my feelings for her. I avoided it and asked inane questions that avoided the elephant in the room.

"How is it Billy Little says he met you in D.C.?"

"I get around. I was just as surprised to see him as he was to see me. Shit happens. That is why I wear wigs and other disguises. I work in a lot of places."

We sat silently for a moment. She kept staring at me. I figured that I might as well get to the obvious.

"Why are you here? Why did you warn me off the gig with Bats? Am I a target? Are you working for Lemmy the Shark?"

"That's a lot of questions. I'll try and explain. This all goes back a lot of years."

"Take your time. It doesn't look like we are going anywhere anytime soon."

I listened and she talked. This is the story she told me.

ELEVEN

Myra sat at the kitchen table sipping oolong tea. Her father Rufus sat across from her. He was a large man. He had a shaved head that held a pair of fierce eyes, a broad nose, and generous lips. His capped teeth shone brilliantly when the light hit them. He had a gentle disarming smile which led many people to not take him as serious as they should have. He blew across the top of his cup. The aroma of his darjeeling laced with honey and whiskey floated across the table to Myra's sensitive nose. She inhaled deeply. Her father looked worried.

"Listen child, we got to have a little talk."

"Sure. Go ahead and talk. I'm all ears."

Her father laughed. "You sure are a feisty one, ain't you? Got it from your mother. Too bad she ain't here. Maybe she could do this better than me. Anyway, I got to get some things straight now that you're old enough to understand. Do you know what I do to make money?"

"Pops, I am not stupid. Why would you think I don't know the score?"

"Because we never talked about it. Because I tried as hard as I could to keep you out of it."

"What, you think I bought that crap that you were always away on business? You think I didn't know who those fat ofay greaseballs were? Come on Pops and give me some credit."

"OK then, miss smarty pants, how about you tell me just what it is that I do."

"Before we get to that, how about we clear some other things up. You think I'm old enough to handle things then let's get some other shit straight. Was my mother really a Crow Indian? I thought it was cool and all but whenever I asked why we never saw any of her family I got a bunch of stories. You know, that she was abandoned and raised by nuns in an orphanage. I mean if she was a Crow Indian then how come she never went to the reservation to look up her parents. How about you tell me just what and who I really am."

"Well Myra, It's like this. You might as well get the straight scoop all at once and then we get it over with. Your mother was no Indian or at least I'm pretty sure she wasn't. I am not sure what she was or why she liked to say she was an Indian. I guess she got off on it and it made her stand out in the clubs. When I met her she was singing and dancing in a joint on the south side. That Indian stuff was all showbiz shit. They billed her as Little Spotted Horse. When we got married she put the name Liza Enescu on the marriage certificate. It must be around here somewhere. Unless she maybe tore it up. We had our ups and downs so I wouldn't blame her if she burned the damn thing. Anyway, she was dark enough to pass for an Indian and she had them funny eyes like you have. She spilled a little one night when she was plastered. Near as I could figure she was some kind of gypsy. Remember how she told you that she was a medicine woman because she could read the tea leaves and tell fortunes? Well, that's all gypsy shit. But then again maybe the gypsy stuff was all made up."

"What? Now I find this out. All my life I'm calling her Little. And what kind of singing and dancing was she doing? I never heard her sing or seen her dance. Well, sometimes we would boogaloo around the house if she was in the mood."

"All right, she was a stripper. And not a very good one. But we hit it off. She wanted to get out of the clubs. She was sick of fighting off the mob guys and all that shit. She also had a junk habit back then. But I took one look and that was that. I was just a street punk in them days. I was running numbers for Greasy Slim Robbie on the west side and hoping to make my way up in the mob."

"Well, I guess you did."

"Yes, I did but not the way I planned. Anyway, we hooked up. She got off the junk, cleaned up, and the next thing we knew you come along. I never saw myself as being daddy material but shit happens."

Myra laughed and then she frowned. "Thanks for that. You are a real piece of work. Sorry I spoiled your plans."

"Oh, come on. It ain't like that. It was just a surprise. Anyway, you turned out just fine."

"Sure I did. So now instead of being some Indian princess like she told me, I'm just a part gypsy nigger child. Ain't that a kick in the head? Funny how I had to put up with all them names and shit as a kid because I told everyone that I was an Indian. And now, in a strange way, it is sort of hip to be an Indian. But maybe what she told you was more bull. Maybe she really was an Indian. I'll believe that. But, you go ahead and fill me in on what you think I think. Even though I think you know what I know unless you think I'm stupid."

"You ain't stupid but I just want to make sure we are clear on things just in case."

"Just in case what? You checking out on me?"

"No but you never know. Stuff happens to guys in my line of work."

"And that line of work is?"

"What do you think I do?"

"I don't think; I know. I told you so. You murder people for that honky slime ball

Lemmy the Shark. I get it. Little and I talked about it. Nobody in the mob ever used a black guy to do hits. Little and I always knew. I give a shit who you kill. They probably all deserve it anyway. But now that we are spilling the secrets, I got some questions. Are these Italians like they show in the movies? Do they show you any respect? I thought they were all full of hate for us moolies."

Rufus laughed out loud. "Sure, some are like that. But see I don't really have anything to do with those guys. How I got recruited is a long story. But what happens is that I get a message. A phone call. Then I go to a drop site. I get the info. If I have to do the trick somewhere else then I get a package with tickets and instructions and pictures and that kind of super spy stuff. I do my work. I make a call. I pick up my money. I never see Lemmy. I have never even met him. If I have to talk to anyone then I see another guy. I don't even know his name. But see sometimes there is no call for my services. That's why I have to do the collections for one of Lemmy's guys. You seen him. Joey Gabs. He runs them juke box and gum machines and stuff. Sometimes people don't pay up on their percentage of the take and I got to remind them that the rent is due. Its small change but it helps when things get slack."

"But here's the thing. I've been lucky. You never know what might go wrong. And if something bad goes down then you might never hear about it. I told Joey Gabs if anything happens to me that he should tell you but who can trust those guys. Lemmy and the big boys won't do shit for you if I get bumped off. I guess I should have tried to put something aside over the years but I didn't. So you got no inheritance to look forward to."

"I never gave it a thought. But I got an idea. First off, I'm going to pretend that I am a real Indian. As a kid I got teased like crazy about the Indian thing but now that being an Indian has some coolness attached I'm going to use it."

"You kind of lost me with all that. I knew finishing high school would do you some good. Me and your mother never got much education."

"It just means it gives me some extra weight. It has some degree of cool. Makes me exotic like it did for Mom when she was in show business."

"Show biz; now that's a laugh. But I gotta say; she was something. She was a real hot number when she was young. So, what you got in mind to do? You going to college? Be a teacher or something?"

"No, you are going to be the teacher. I want you to show me how to do what you do. See, you being a black guy doing hits for the mob makes it unusual. But feature a half black half Indian girl doing hits. Who would ever suspect that? I'll tell you who; no one."

Rufus swallowed hard. He coughed. "Are you crazy, girl?"

"No, I been giving this a lot of thought. So either you teach me or I'll find someone who will. Up to you, Daddy dear."

"And here I was thinking maybe you would be the one to set what's left of this bad ass family on the straight path. I don't know why but I kind of seen you settling down and raising some kids with a nice professional man. I could set out on the front porch and put my grandchillin's on my knee."

"You must be smokin' the evil weed, Daddy. You got the wrong girl. I've been studying. Not what you think but stuff like etiquette and manners and fashion and vocabulary. I figure if I have to run around the country wiping out bad guys then I have to learn to fit in anywhere I am. I been reading them James Bond books."

"Well, hell Myra. Why don't you join the CIA or FBI and do that kind of stuff legit?"

"They are not going to hire a girl especially a girl like me. And what happens when they do background checks? Come on, you must be kidding."

"Yeah, I guess you got a point. Well, little girl, I got to say I ain't happy about your career choices but if that is what you want to do then you got the right man to show you the ropes. I suppose it is the only thing of value that I got to pass on down to you. Even if you change your mind, and I hope you do, then ain't no one in this life going to mess with you. I see you got the heart and the will but I'm goin' to make sure you got the smarts. Talkin' about snuffin' out a guy is one thing. Doin' it is another. But I got to tell you goin' in that you don't get to pick and choose. You got to hit who you are told to hit. Now I ain't never had to off any kids but there have been a few women. I don't like it but I figure if the big man wants somebody gone then he got a good reason. You got to think like a soldier in a war. These people are just targets. It is them or you. Difference is that they don't know that. But you'll see what I mean. But you won't know if this is for you until that first time when you got to do the deed. Up until then it's just all shuck and jive. It's how steady that finger on that trigger is when the time comes. It's about how you breathe and sweat and stay steady. Maybe you got the nerves and maybe you don't. I sure never saw this coming. But like I said: even if you don't take to this stuff when we are finished you are going to be one dangerous redskin."

Myra smiled and then started laughing. Rufus laughed along with her. She was thrilled and happy. Rufus was scared but hid it from his strange and beautiful child.

Oh man, he thought to himself. If only Little were here to see what she done raised.

TWELVE

I felt my hands clutching the arms of the chair I was seated in. I stared at Myra. Was any of this story she was spinning to be believed? Was I supposed to buy that Lemmy the Shark was using a black chick to do his dirty work? Even the fact that he had been using a black guy was a real stretch. It was hard to swallow. I snapped out of my internal doubts and started peppering her with questions. I needed answers. I had been in some crazy scenes but this scenario was hard to get a grip on. I could see her as Lemmy's squeeze or even moving drugs for him but a hit man? Just what kind of crazy movie was I in the middle of?

"How is it you were in D.C.? Why did you warn me off the gig with Bats? How do you even know Bats? Just what the hell is going on?"

"Ease up, Thorny," she said with a slight grin on her face. "You look like a scared kid who just got caught with his hand in the cookie jar. I know it's a lot to take in but that is just the way it is. I had a job to do in D.C. I'm a jazz fan. I heard about Billy and the band. I didn't know he was playing here tonight. No big deal. We're cool. As for the rest, well that's another thing. Let me go back a little. I learned from Rufus. He took me on a hit when he thought I was ready. I got to admit that I was a natural. Nobody knew about me. About six years ago Rufus and I got caught in a set-up. It was some rival mob shit between Chicago and Philly. I lost my Pops. I got away. Back in Chicago I called Pops contact. He had trouble buying my story but he got word about me to Lemmy. He was curious about me. I convinced Joey Gabs to let me take over Pops deal. Things went well and I ain't looked back until now."

I was listening but I was still having a hard time accepting her story. I looked up. Her expression, deadpan up until now, changed. Her eyes drifted upward and to the right. She was remembering something. She got up and started pacing.

"I just had my birthday. I'm forty. I know I don't look it but I am. I started getting odd vibes that I've never had before. When we met and danced something hit me. I got new feelings. I thought I had no feelings. But you holding me just woke something up in me. I got scared. You left and I was there with Linko at the club. What a pig he is. And then it started to hit me what pigs they all were. I wanted something different. I went home. For the first time in years I was sitting on the john and crying. I don't cry, I don't ever cry. Like I said, something is happening. I waited. I bided my time. Then you called. We went to Milwaukee. I was afraid of what I felt and what I knew about the shit you were about to get into. That's why I slugged you. But I couldn't let you go down. I just couldn't."

"What the hell are you talking about?"

She waved her hands in the air. She looked around the room as if she expected something to jump out at her. Her eyes blinked. She exhaled. She never looked more beautiful. I moved to the edge of my seat. She turned to me.

"Your pal Bats pissed off the wrong people. The trucking company moves product for Lemmy. It ain't records and shit that has been shorted and that they think is being stolen, it's drugs. I'm supposed to take out the owner. But see Joey Gabs got it in for Bats from some old crap between them from years ago. So he gets Lemmy to let him bring in Bats on a job. I do the owner but Bats gets the blame. Joey Gabs, who is a real nasty prick, figures Bats will get sent up and he can have his guys in stir take care of him. Meanwhile, I get my cash and head for Cabo for a few weeks. But I find out from Joey Gabs that your idiot pal ropes you in on this deal and tells Joey Gabs to let you take the fall after the hits. You think that he's a friend but the plan was to leave you holding the bag. So I get word to take care of both the owner and to set you up along with Bats. Like I told you, this would not normally bother me. More hits means extra cash in my bank account. But I couldn't do it. So I warned you off. I am not sure what to do now. I have money and a passport. The hit isn't until next week. The plan is to get word to Bats about a truck and where to follow it. It's a drug drop off and a meet between Jenkins and a supplier. It's all bogus. I'm supposed to be there to do the guy and you and leave Bats to take the fall. It's all set up with the local sheriff who is on Lemmy's pad. So that's my story."

"You have got to be kidding, Myra. I'm glad you fell for me and warned me off. I guarantee that the feeling is mutual but this is a ton of shit you are laying on me all at once. I learn that the dame I'm hot for is a hit man, my pal is ready to set me up to take the fall for murder, and you are supposed to off the both of us. Now you want me to tell you what we should do. How about if I just let my head explode?"

She came up to me. She pulled me up. She took my head in her hands. She kissed me like I have never been kissed before. I felt her fear and her desperation. Or maybe those were my feelings. Jesus, what the hell was I supposed to do now? I was holding Lemmy the Shark's hitman. She felt right in my arms but everything else felt wrong. She tightened her grip on me. I felt her urgency.

I was scared shitless. I needed help. I pushed her away. I held her at arms length. I tried to speak. Nothing came out. Her eyes looked into mine. I found my voice.

"What are we going to do? Or what are you going to do??"

Myra started pacing the small room. Her head was bobbing up and down. She stopped and turned to me.

"Sit down," she said. "I have an idea. Let's go back to the club and catch Billy's last set. I've got to work out a few things and the music helps me think."

I was blown away by her coolness. My mind was all in a jumble while she now seemed totally at ease. I began to understand why she was such a successful assassin. I was jumping out of my skin and she just wanted to catch a few more sounds. I followed her down the stairs not unlike a cow being led to slaughter. I could only hope that following her would not lead to an air hammer to my forehead.

PART TWO

THIRTEEN

The sky was a solid gray. The little light that managed to filter through the solid ceiling of clouds seemed almost other worldly. It was as if God was holding back the day. The sand on the beach was also gray. It felt damp underfoot from the humidity. At first glance it looked dirty. It wasn't. The temperature was warm. The air was heavy. It was infused with the refuse-laden odors of the city. Not many people were to be seen walking on the beach. None were entering the polluted water. It was late morning on a Wednesday. The huge city of Lima hovered in the background like a ravenous dog ready to consume what little was left of any open space. It was a city that was almost modern in the center and trendy in the wealthy suburbs. But above it all stood the crumbling hillsides dotted with the encampments of the poor. They stood in silent witness to the ravages of a failed economy. It was the result of centuries of being plundered by other nations and its own ruling class. Many of the so-called homes consisted of nothing more than four poles and a piece of plastic thrown over them. There was no running water. There was no power except what could be stolen by tapping into power lines. The sendero luminoso, the shining path, were left wing terrorists trying to overthrow the corrupt regime. Shootings and explosions were commonplace. Peru was imperiled on all sides and yet life went on. Police armed with automatic weapons were everywhere. They cared little about street crime and stood by while relentless pick pockets plied their trade. They were there only to kill any suspected anti government rebels. Despite this the city was alive and active. Prices were cheap especially if you had American money. The local food was plentiful and delicious. Rents were almost silly in their affordability. What was once the glorious Inca civilization had descended into a banana republic.

Thornell Pilsudski left the beach and returned to his apartment. He now stood bare-chested on the spacious balcony overlooking the cloud covered churning Pacific. He turned around. He looked at the rumpled empty bed. A soft breeze blew the lace curtains beside the window and caused them to billow around his body. He frowned. He took a deep breath of the salty sea air. After six months he still found it hard to believe that he was in this place and living the life that he was living. Never in a million years could he have imagined what his existence had now become. He turned once again to the empty bed and wished that he could see Myra, in the bed sleeping. His heart swelled not only with love but gratitude and with wonder. As he did so often he began to uncoil the events that had led him to this foreign land. The pieces fell into place. How Myra had pulled off what she did still left him thrilled and amazed. The events once again began to play out in his mind. It had begun while they sat and listened to Billy Little and his band do their final set. Stippy and Berta were on the balcony above them. The room was swollen with a huge late-night crowd. Smoke and chatter filled the air. Billy was wailing away on a Miles tune. He was doing runs that sent chills up Thorny's spine despite his worry about what was coming his way.

Myra leaned close to Thorny. She began speaking into his left ear. He listened with a combination of fear and wonder. The next week would prove to be an experience that he hoped to never have to endure again.

FOURTEEN

Later that night, after the band finished and the club closed, Thorny lay in the bed in the garage apartment behind Stippy Kowalski's restaurant. He rested on his side. He watched as Myra slept. He was mesmerized by the slight swelling of her magnificent breasts as she breathed. A broad smile spread across his face as he recalled the night's lovemaking. He knew she was special but he had no idea just how special. After she had told him of her plan on how to extricate both of them from the deal he had made with Bats and her assignment from Lemmy, they had fallen into bed. The fury of her passion had left him drained. Myra was a woman unlike any he had ever known. He was not sure that what she had put before him was workable or even reasonable. He didn't care. If what she wanted to do would leave them free and together than he would go along without any hesitation. It was a simple plan but there some moving parts. There was also no return if it all went well. This move meant giving up everything he ever knew. He had been involved in any number of shady deals but nothing like this was ever foreseen by him. It sounded like a plot from one of the fantasy novels he used to read as a teenager.

Myra rolled over on her side facing away from him. Her muscled alabaster back lay exposed. He leaned over. He took in a deep breath. He kissed her between her shoulder blades. She stirred. She turned to him. Her eyes opened. She smiled. His heart swelled. He gathered her in his arms. He felt her strength. He threw off the sheets. He rose up and entered her. He thought that he would melt. They were both smiling as he rose and fell. He kissed her full moist lips as he exploded inside her.

What would be a new life or the last chapter in his twisted career was about to begin.

FIFTEEN

The phone rang 8 times before Thorny
heard the receiver being lifted off its cradle,
No voice answered. What he heard was a
series of loud coughs and swear words
followed by more coughing.

"Who the hell is this?" mumbled Bats.

"It's me, dick head."

"Thorny? What the fuck? My old lady
says you called and said you were screwing
me over. What the hell is going on? I
thought we were all set."

"Your wife must have a brain that's
gone haywire. I told her I had to be out of
town on a job over the weekend. I'm all set
for whenever this thing is taking place."

"Shit, you had me worried. I'm just
waiting for a call. As soon as I get the word,
I'll let you know. Should be a breeze. All we
got to do is follow this truck and see where
he unloads the merch. I give the word to the

boss about what we see on this operation and we collect the dough. Easy as pie. No need for hardware or shit like that."

"If this is nothing but a tail job then what do you need me for? Something ain't kosher about this deal? What are you not telling me?"

"Jesus, what is it with you? I already explained that they know my face around the shipping company. They could spot me tailing them. You drive and I wear a mask or sit in the back or something. We don't want to spook these guys. They could just pass up the dump off spot. I want to get this thing over quick. I am tapped out and I need the cash now. See, I get this done right and then maybe other jobs line up. I'll cut you in. Maybe word gets out and we get a rep. You know, like fixers. The mob likes to stay clean these days. They want to be seen as legit businessmen. They want to send their kids to fancy shmancy schools and play golf at the South Shore Country Club and shit like that. So maybe they see old Bats as the guy to go to."

"Sure, whatever you say, Bats. Just call me with as much heads up time as you can. I assume you got a car for us to use."

"You got it, Thorny. I'll be in touch. Stay cool."

Myra smiled. She had been listening in on the conversation.

"Some buddy you got there. It's a wonder he has stayed alive this long being so stupid."

"Bats may not be too smart but he one time saved my life. I owe him even if he is planning on selling me out. When this goes down please let me deal with him."

"I can't promise anything. If he starts anything then I am going to finish it. Someone who is going to send me down the river has to pay in my book. You have a sentimental side that makes you kind of endearing. I like it but it can get you killed. I'll handle things. Just stay close to the phone. This thing will probably be going down in a couple of days. I got to see Joey Gabs tonight. Now give me a kiss."

Thorny did as he was told. The way she held him made him weak in the knees.

After Myra left he started thinking about Bats betrayal. It tied his stomach in knots. The tenuous control that he had over his highly compromised world had started to veer off track. He thought about Myra. When he stared into her glistening dark eyes after she kissed him he had felt reassured. That should have been enough to erase all his doubts. But it wasn't.

SIXTEEN

"So this is it?" I asked. "We follow this truck until it stops to pick up the stuff? And then what?"

"Don't worry," said Bats. "I'll take care of everything. You just keep this baby running."

At this point I wasn't sure where we were. I figured it was some back road outside of Elgin. I was keeping close enough to not lose sight of the truck but far enough back so that he didn't spot us following him. I figured Myra was somewhere behind me but if she was, I didn't spot her.

I had to hit the brakes when the truck slowed and turned off onto a narrow dirt road. It was pitch black. The night was cloudy. The air smelled of dampness and mold. I shivered.

"This must be the exchange place." Bats whispered. "I figure they are going to off load part of the haul. You stay with the car until I signal you with the flashlight."

Bats reached behind the seat and came up with a sawed off shotgun. He broke it open and made sure the dual chambers were loaded. He got out of the car and started down the road. I had the lights off and was parked off the road under a tree. I heard a car pull up behind me. I got out of the car and saw Myra coming toward me. She was all in black. She had a revolver in each hand. She put one of the pistols up against her mouth cautioning me not to speak. She came close.

"Listen to me. You are going to hear a few gun shots. That will be the driver catching it. Bats will give you the signal. When you walk in there the shit is going to hit the fan. Either Joey Gabs is going to do the killing or Bats will. I am not sure just what Gabs is going to do. He may want to let Bats do you. I couldn't get a clear picture but this is what is going to happen. I am going to lead you in at gun point. I am going to tell you to get down on the ground. Just do it. Don't hesitate. Do you understand?"

"Of course I do. But what are you going to do?"

"Just do what I say. Or maybe its better you stay here and let me handle things. I don't know if you're equipped to deal with what needs to be done."

"I'm not sure I like the sound of that."

"Listen to me. We got the plan and it was all laid out to you. Don't back out now, Thorny. Don't push me into a corner I don't want to be in."

My stomach knotted up. Sure I was deep into Myra but she also scared me. I did not want to find out what she would do if I balked at this point. I said nothing and simply nodded. We set off down the road.

As we turned past a huge elm we saw four men standing in the glare of the trucks headlights. Two of the men had their hands in the air. Joey Gabs was holding a pistol on them. Bats stood to the side.

Myra pushed me forward. I stumbled.

"Down," she yelled. I fell forward. Gunshots filled the air. I kept my face buried in the dirt. I heard screams. There was more gun fire. I felt my leg being kicked.

"Get up, Thorny," Myra said. I rose slowly. I brushed the dirt off my pants. I looked around. The same two men were leaning against the truck with their backs to us. Bats and Joey Gabs lay in the grass. They were not moving. I ran over to Bats. Blood was coming out of his mouth. I leaned over him.

"Jesus, Bats. You hurt bad?"

He forced a smile. Blood covered his teeth and seeped out of the corners of his mouth.

"Sorry. No choice. Tell my old lady. It was you or me. What could I do?"

He coughed and was gone.

I turned back to Myra. She shook her head.

"I had to do it, Thorny. I had to kill Joey Gabs and Bats threw down on me. Now we got to get going. This is not the time for regrets or second thoughts. We do not have much time."

I stood rooted in place. Despite her warnings I was really unprepared for this. She took me by the arm and led me to where the two men were standing. She tapped one of them on the head with her gun.

"Do you two know what is in the truck?"

"Look, lady," said the man. He was wearing a torn jacket and had on a cloth cap. He was heavy set and looked to be a well-worn 50 or so years old. "All we do is drive. We was told to stop here and that some people would remove some stuff from the truck. We were then supposed to continue on to Milwaukee and drop things off. We were told we would be paid off then we were on our own. All we know is that we got a load of records, tapes, and cassettes. That's it. We never seen the two dead guys or you or him before. We don't want no trouble. We got wives and kids. I don't wanna' die."

"Relax. You and your partner are not going to die. Unlock the back and open the doors. Hurry up."

They did as they were told. Myra handed me one of her pistols.

"Keep an eye on these two. If they move then shoot them."

I nodded. Myra crawled up into the truck.

"Look, mister," said the man in the cap. "Let us go. You don't look like no killer. That bitch is nuts. She shot those two guys before they could even say anything. What the hell is she looking for? Just turn around and we'll beat it."

"Shut up," I said. "Just sit down the both of you. You'll be fine."

Myra threw a duffel bag out of the truck. She jumped down after it. She picked up the bag and came towards me.

"We have to go." She looked at the two men on the ground.
"You men get up in the back of the truck. You wait an hour. Then you can do what ever you want. Remember; I know who you are. You do anything other than what I told you then I will find you and kill you and your whole family. Do you understand what I'm telling you?"

We walked back to her car. My head was spinning. She put the bag in the trunk. She backed the car out and we sped off into the night. I was numb. I was sick over seeing Bats die. She had told me this might happen. But, still I was unprepared for it. We were headed west. Myra reached over and squeezed my knee. She turned to me and smiled.

"Things are going to move fast now. You did what I said. Didn't you? You have your passport? You dumped that old beater of yours?"

"Jesus, Myra. That was cold. Did you have to kill Bats? Wasn't there some other way? Would you really kill those two drivers and their families?"

"Listen to me, Thorny. I told you what might happen. It's over. They were going to kill us. OK, so things did not go exactly as I thought they would. But that's Lemmy's way. We are out of it now. I have to lay off the drugs. The cash will set us up. A few more days and we will be in Canada. I meet my connection and we are off to South America. A new life. Come on. We'll be just like Jack and Neal. On the road. Hell, just turn the page. A new chapter. Screw the old shit. With my connections and our skill sets my Peruvian pals will keep us busy. Down there we will be like royalty. And it is warm. The people are great, the food is great and the living is easy. There must be 50 pounds of blow in that bag. It'll fetch a pretty penny. We got it made in the shade. Rufus and Little would be mighty proud of their daughter. Aren't you proud of me? I told you I had a plan and I did. Now lean over here and give me a smootch. The worst part is over. And no, I would not kill those guys and their families. Well, not unless I absolutely had to."

I did as I was told. I kissed her cheek. I sat back. I was numb. What the hell was I into now?

SEVENTEEN

"Look, kiddo. This shit is hotter than a pistol. I will have to lay this bundle off in small pieces. I suddenly dump this weight in this area and Lemmy will catch wind and I got big trouble. I don't need trouble of any size let alone Lemmy size trouble. Things are hot enough around here now. And before you say another word, don't think I'm stupid. This stuff has got to be Lemmy's so don't give me any bull shit. That is who you work for so where the hell else would you get this dope from. I'll give you this; you got a pair on you. Wasn't offin' guys payin' enough? You gonna' roll the dice on this one shot? Lemmy got a long reach. You sure you wanna' do this?"

We were standing inside a freezing barn somewhere in Wisconsin. The man in front of us had a long bushy beard. He kept spitting tobacco juice. He was fat and dressed in a dirty pair of coveralls. Myra called him Butch. I did not like the way he looked at us.

"Save the shit for someone else, Butch," said Myra. "I told you what was coming and we agreed on a deal. And just how the fuck do you know what I do for Lemmy?"

"Sure, kiddo; that we did. But I never figured on this weight. And I sure didn't figure it to be Lemmy's shit so maybe I'm as dumb as you are. You must be dumb if you didn't know the word was out on Lemmy's Indian gunhand."

"Come off it. It don't matter. Who the hell did you think I was going to rip off? You know the score. So quit trying to jerk me around. Give me my price. We can't be hanging around here much longer. If you know about me then everyone else must know."

Butch looked at me. He smiled with a mouth half empty of teeth. He shrugged. He looked at me and grinned.

"She is a piece of work, ain't she? Just like her old man."

"She sure is," I said. "So maybe we wind this up before she gets annoyed and I freeze to death. I've seen her annoyed. It ain't pretty."

"Yeah, I imagine it ain't. OK, listen. I got a car for you. Full up. Clean plates. You should have no problem wherever you two are headed. I'll give you the car and 50 grand. I'm going to have to sit on this pile for a long time. You know Lemmy ain't going to rest."

Myra laughed. "A hundred, you cheap shit. There is a half a mil in there once you cut it and you know it. Now quit dicking around and give me the cash."

Butch looked at the ground. He shook his head. He spit a wad of something out. He kicked some dirt. He looked up and smiled.

"OK, you got it. But it's only because I knew your old man. I'll go 60."

"You'll go a hundred and here is why. If you don't I will take it and leave. Then I'll call Lemmy and tell him you were behind the whole thing. I'll tell him you got word of what was going down. I'll tell him you did Joey Gabs. Who you think he'll believe? You wanna' take that chance or you want to pay up and get us out of your hair? So you sit on the shit for awhile. It'll be like a retirement fund you can't tap until you retire. Now give me my price or we walk."

"You won't do that. You do and you are going to have to explain what happened and where the dope is. Don't bullshit the bull shitter, Myra. Take the 60 and get out before I change my mind."

"Screw you, Butch. Give me my hundred or I'll blow out your kneecaps."

Butch's eyes widened. He looked around for help. Myra had her pistol out.

"You pull that trigger, little girl, and six of my guys will be here before you can turn around."

"So what? You'll be dead. If I don't get my money then I don't care what happens."

"Myra," I said. "How about we take his offer and get out? Isn't 60 grand enough?"

"No, it is not. Now get me a hundred out of that safe you got buried under that horse stall over there or I am going to shoot you to pieces one bullet at a time. We had a deal, Butch. Don't try and treat me like some damn mook. You got no fucking idea of what I can do with this pistol."

Butch shook his large hairy head. "OK, fuck it. You can't blame a guy for trying to deal a little. You know how it goes, kiddo. Shit, I used to bounce you on my knee."

"Sure you did. Thanks for the sweet trip down memory lane but you just get in that stall, open that trap door and give me my cash or the only thing bouncing around here will be my bullets bouncing off your skull. You've weighed and tasted the blow. You know it's good. Move it."

I stood guard while Myra followed Butch into a horse stall at the back of the barn. I could not see what was going on. I was peeking through the barn slats to make sure no one was heading our way. In a few minutes I turned to see Butch walking towards me. Myra was behind him. She had her pistol in his back. In her left hand was a small case.

"Nice doing biz, Butch. You got the shit and we are taking off. Do what you want. It might be a good idea to give the shit back to Lemmy. Put you in good with him."

"Sure, kiddo, but then I'll be out a hundred G's. I don't figure a shit like Lemmy will cover my loss, do you?"

"You never know. Most likely he will take the blow and have you shot. But you do what you want. Now just to make sure you don't have your boys try and stop us, you are going for a little ride with us. I'll drop you off once we are down the road a ways."

"Hey, this ain't part of no deal I made."

"Shut up, Butch and get your stinky ass in the car."

Myra motioned for me to put the restraints that I always carried with me on Butch. Once I did that we pushed him into the back seat of the tan Chevy Nova he was trading us for Myra's stolen car. We headed off his property. We passed some of his men but when they saw Butch in the back seat they just walked away. Myra let him out of the car once we were a couple of miles down the road.

Butch stood red-faced at the side of the road.

"You better not come back this way, kiddo. Rufus daughter or not, you are dead meat if I find you."

"No worries, Butch. You take care and have a nice walk."

Myra put the car in gear and we headed north.

"So far, so good," said Myra. She had a big grin on her face. "And now for a nice leisurely trip across Canada. My pals will be waiting in Vancouver. You ever been to Canada, Thorny?"

"No, I have not. Just what do you have in store for us there, Myra? And what is this stuff about Peru?"

"Oh, you are gonna' love it. Just leave things to me."

And, amazingly, I did.

EIGHTEEN

I had always imagined Canada to be a strange cold place with a bunch of small towns and huskies and Mountie's. I was just a little wrong. Sure we passed a lot of empty prairie and farm land. But we hit some big cities that were just like in the USA but a lot cleaner. It was when we hit Vancouver that I was really surprised. It was beautiful. By the time we got there Myra and I were well rested, well fed, and just about screwed out. Every time she looked at that stash of greenbacks she got horny. I had been on a lot of road trips but this one was the tops. We must have broken in half the motel beds in the Great White North.

We ditched the car way outside the city. We took the train into the city center. Myra checked us into a fancy hotel by the water. Once in the room she threw herself on the bed and began laughing.

"Isn't life grand, Thorny? This is the best thing I ever did. Rufus made a good living but what happened in the end? It was time to get out. This money will buy us a new life and it is going to be the cat's ass. You just wait and see. I got to make a call. Then let's go out and get some new clothes. Everything we have has to go. We start fresh."

I looked down at her spread out on the huge bed.

"Myra, you are something else. I still can't believe this is happening. I mean South America? What the hell am I going to do there? What are we going to do?"

She jumped off the bed. "Don't you worry. I got it all planned. You'll understand when you meet my pals. See, something I have not told you is that my work was not only in the states. Rufus and I worked for people other than Lemmy and the Chicago boys. We got all kinds of back door offers for our services. Just you wait. You have been cross-country cruisin' with an international celeb."

Myra started jumping up and down on the bed. She leapt off and grabbed me in a tight bear hug.

"I feel free, Thorny. No more Lemmy. No more having to deal with those fat grease balls. Our new friends have much better manners and a lot more class. Of course their methods are a little different from ours. It takes a little getting used to but, you know, when in Rome."

"I can't wait to meet these new friends. I somehow have the feeling that they are no angels. Are you sure we will be safe with them? Do I dare ask just what it is that you do for them? Never mind. What am I thinking? I guess no matter where you are in the world there is always somebody who wants somebody else done away with. But why you? Surely these guys must have their own assassins."

"What a fancy word for my line of work. You'll soon understand. I can go places that they can't. Plus they do not want any trails leading back to them. But no worries. You'll see. Now go get cleaned up and let's hit the stores. I need a new dress and some new shoes. Lets get properly attired and then hit the town."

I stood under the shower and began to wonder just how I had gotten into this. It was as if I had been swept up into a tornado, spun around, and dropped on the west coast of Canada. I had abandoned my whole existence and was now going to follow a professional killer to South America and a life I knew nothing about. What seemed like a good idea just a few days ago now seemed a little crazy. OK, a lot crazy. It was as if my will had gone into a deep slumber. Myra was so positive that I only doubted things when I was away from her. That was not often. Well, I thought, there is no going back now. I felt bad about not calling Bats wife. I just could not bring myself to do it. I figured she would get the news from the cops. I wanted to call her. I figured that no matter what had happened, that I owed it to her. But when the time came I could not do it. What could I say? He was a rat? He was going to let me take a fall for his shit? Maybe he was going to get me killed? That my lover shot him? Best, I figured, to just let the past go. Forget the life I once had. Myra was right. On to the next chapter. Shit, I always wanted to learn Spanish. I knew some from high school.

"Hey, save me some hot water," Myra yelled from the bedroom.

I stepped out of the shower. Her naked body swept past me with a quick kiss. I grinned. I shook my head in wonder. She was truly something else.

* *

Myra spun around in her new dress. She looked great. The hotel concierge had called ahead to a couple of stores so that when we arrived they were all ready for us. Myra dropped some heavy coin but we were outfitted like the classiest pair of gringos in Vancouver. We even found a jazz club in Gastown. Of all people Brubeck was there. Now that was a treat. No one has quite the sound that Paul Desmond coaxes from his sax.

Myra told me that we would be meeting some of her people the next day. I was looking forward to who she was going to have me meet. I fell asleep with all sorts of wild shit running through my head. Had she done hits for the Peruvian mafia? Was there a Peruvian mafia? She said it was better if I knew nothing until we were safely out of the country. I was not happy when she said the less I knew then the less I could reveal under duress. I did not like the sound of that. This was beginning to sound like CIA shit. The last thing I wanted was any more of the Feds. My time in the army had left me with a bitter taste when it came to the government. They played dirty. But if they were in with Myra then we were probably beyond any conventional accountability. I blew it all away. What the hell would the CIA want with Myra? I guess I would soon find out. I looked over at Myra's sleeping face. My but she was a beautiful woman. She looked almost angelic when asleep. She might be an avenging angel, a dangerous deadly angel but still an angel in repose.

NINETEEN

We were seated in a private room. It was
upstairs of a restaurant located on the
outskirts of the city. We had entered by way
of an alley. We walked through the kitchen
of what seemed like a giant Chinese
restaurant. We climbed two sets of wooden
stairs until we entered the room we were
now in. Seated at a large square table was a
portly man in a three piece suit. Across from
him was a woman who looked like a body
builder. She sported a buzz cut hairdo. She
was in short sleeves and loose trousers.
Standing behind her were two bruisers who,
I assumed, were her muscle. The minute we
entered the room she leapt up and rushed to
Myra. They embraced like long lost family.
They started chattering away in rapid
Spanish. My high school exposure to the
language, dimly remembered, was no match.
I could hardly catch a stray word. The fat

man sat and stared with a disgusted look on his face. Myra turned to me.

"Thorny, this is Adela. We have worked together before. I have explained that we are a team and work as a unit."

She turned to the seated man in the suit.

"Colonel Navarett," she said. "It is good to see you once again. I hope all is well with you and your family."

The man stood and gave a small bow in our direction. He began to speak in Spanish. Myra stood at rigid attention while she listened with an expressionless face. When he finished he sat back down. I looked at Myra. She did not look happy.

"I understand your feelings but I assure you that we will do only as you and Adela ask. Remember, I do not come empty handed."

I smiled at the Colonel. He ignored me. I looked to Myra.

"This, Thorny, is Colonel Navarett. He is the head of the unit that acts to protect the Peruvian government against all problems both foreign and domestic. Adela heads up a unit that carries out whatever needs to be done. I did a couple of jobs for them when they needed a foreign national. It's all very on the down low. The Colonel, despite his disdain for my methods, has to accept the reality of certain situations. It seems that my services or I should say our services are once again needed."

"Are you kidding? You mean we are leaving home to act as assassins for a foreign government? Do they understand what you are saying?"

The Colonel rose once again. "We all speak English. Please take a seat. My objections to your use have been noted but I am once again over ruled. Adelita seems to have the president's ear to a far greater degree than I do. Since it is all in service to our nation, I must go along. Please be seated and we will explain what is needed and how we think you may go about achieving our objectives. Sadly our own hands are tied due to interference from your nation's CIA and the objections of the Mexicans. You Americans seem to think that we exist only to serve your national and economic interests. The fate of all the Latin countries seems to be beside the point. Every time we approach self sufficiency your people rush in with assassination squads. Our needs and our concerns are always ignored. If we show anything but subservience to your needs and wishes then we are cast aside. But one day things will change. Fidel is just the start. Sadly they have now become dependant on the Russians which is unfortunate. We have other plans. I am only here to reassure you that, despite my misgivings, you are now working for Adela and her group. I wish you luck and hope to see you both in Lima in the not too distant future."

I stood with my mouth hanging open. The Colonel rose and left the room. I could not believe what I had just heard. I thought the 100 grand was simply buying us a safe haven in a foreign land. I had no idea that Myra had enlisted us as members of Peru's secret hit squads. But I guess I should have known what was coming. How else would Myra have become so close to these people if it was not through her work as a hit man? I had really stepped into it this time. I sat down. Myra and Adela were once again hugging and laughing. The muscle boys seemed to be relaxed now that the Colonel was gone. I was beginning to wonder what the hell I was doing in this place. Things had been moving so fast that I had not really thought about my future. Was I now to be Myra's back-up partner in our own little Murder Incorporated venture? I could hardly use the investigative skills I had in foreign places where I did not speak the language. Maybe I would have been better off taking my chances on the turf where I knew my way around. Or maybe I should try and stay in Canada. At least they spoke English.

I heard Adela say something. The two muscle boys lifted me out of my chair.

"Myra has filled me in on how you two came to us," Adela said. "These two men are part of my team. Raul and Ernesto. They have limited English. Come, let us go downstairs and eat. I am sure you are hungry. The food here is exceptional although far different from the chifas in my country. Myra can tell you. Come, it is time we get acquainted. Tomorrow we will discuss what we have in mind for you. And then we leave this frozen land."

TWENTY

I sat looking out the window of the Lear jet. Vancouver faded into the mist of a thick cloud cover. The muscle boys were asleep. Myra and Adela were jabbering away in Spanish. My mind was a jumble. I had never felt so out of control. What ever had come my way back home was always something I could manage to handle. I knew the streets. I had contacts. I was now flying to a strange land without a clue as to what I was going to face. Adela had given us phony passports. They identified us as Mexicans. They looked real. I could only guess as to why we did not get Peruvian passports. I was hoping that Myra would fill me in later as to what the hell was going on. Once again I doubted if I was doing the right thing. When we crossed the tarmac at the small airport outside Vancouver, I almost bolted for the bushes. It was only Myra's firm grip on my arm and her smile that kept me going up the stairs and into the plane. Well, there was no turning back now. All I could think of was that Sinatra tune about llama land and a one man band. Come fly with me, indeed.

* * *

That was then and this was now. The six months in Peru had sped by quickly. Aside from the intensive Spanish classes, both Thorny and Myra were trained in the use of the Peruvian weapons. They also had physical training along with lessons in spy craft. They were treated well and fed well.

The city had a lot to offer. They were also taken on a trip to Macchu Picchu and spent weekends at local resorts. Thorny had grown to love the Peruvian food. The fish was exceptional and all the different kinds of potatoes were a revelation. He even learned to like ceviche.

The language came much easier for Thorny than all the physical exercises. He was not used to so much expenditure of effort. But when he stood naked in front of the bathroom mirror, he liked what he saw. He also got to spend some time with the local police so as to familiarize him with the methods they used. He soon realized that cops were the same everywhere. Only everything was magnified in Peru. The pay was dismal so bribery and corruption was taken as a given. The unchecked brutality was also on a scale that made Chicago look tame. Everything was jacked up even more due to the shining path rebel forces and their bombings.

Both Myra and Thorny avoided Americans as much as possible. They stuck to their Mexican identities and kept as low a profile as possible. Thorny was still not sure what they were being trained for. Everything was very hush-hush. Myra told him that the Peruvian's played everything close to the vest. When they were ready they would tell them who or what the target was and then things would move very fast. Myra was anxious for some action. She was used to doing things her way. Being under constant surveillance and supervision by the local secret service was beginning to get on her nerves.

Myra had filled Thorny in on her previous jobs for Adela. A trip down the Amazon. A quick kill. A FIFO job in the Chilean wine country. She knew something big was in the works but she had no idea what it was.

Thorny and Myra only spoke Spanish now. All the training had intensified in the past couple of weeks. They knew they were getting close to learning what was going to be expected of them.

Thorny turned towards the sound of the door to their apartment squeaking open. They left the squeaky hinges without oil as an early warning system. Myra walked in. She was dressed in a colorful short dress. She was smiling. Thorny took her in his arms and kissed her. She whispered into his ear.

"It is on. We are to meet on Monday at the safe house in Miraflores. It is about time. Now we earn our pay. Lucky I still have my Ruger. These damn Sigs can jam."

Thorny stood back. "What pay? We paid them. All we have so far is free rent and food. And all the training. So, what do you think the job will be? I hope it doesn't involve torture. I am not up for that."

Myra laughed. "Don't be such a pussy. That is not our thing. What we do is quick and over in the blink of an eye. We'll find out what the play is. Meanwhile Adela has set us up with a weekend at Playa Azul. Remember that resort we went to. I love those anticuchos they make there. We get in a little R & R and then get ready. You got to admit, Thorny, this beats the hell out of your small time shit back in Chicago. All this training has been good for you. You look really healthy. A regular Charles Atlas. Nobody on the beach is going to be kicking sand in your face."

We both laughed. Myra laughed with anticipation. My laughter was much more a matter of nerves.

TWENTY-ONE

The barracks room lacked air conditioning. The day was warm. The room smelled of floor wax and Lysol. Myra and Thorny sat across a table from Adela and two uniformed officers they had never seen before.

"Let us begin," said Adela. "These two men will give you the background on your target. Please open the folders in front of you."

Thorny looked down at a black and white photo of a man in an ill-fitting suit. He had fleshy jowls, a large mustache, and small porcine eyes.

"That," said Adela, "is Antonio Cienfuego's. He is a member of Fidel's inner circle. We have proof that he has been funneling money and weapons to the rebels her in Lima. We have not found out who his contact is here. We will eventually but in the meantime he must be removed. So far he has been almost impossible to get to."

Myra stood up. "Hold on, Adela. I hope you are not saying you want us to sneak into Cuba and eliminate this guy. There is not much I won't do but going into Cuba is one of them. I have heard what happens to people if they get hold of you."

Adela raised her hand. Thorny could see the calluses on her fingers. Sometimes he found it hard to believe Adela was really a woman. Her short hair and stocky build made her look like a wrestler. Even her voice was as deep as a mans. He wondered what her two body guards could do that she couldn't do herself.

"No, of course not, Myra. You two would not last five minutes in Havana. We have learned that he is being invited by the Mexican government to the grand opening of a new private resort in Cancun. A number of Latin American dignitaries have been invited. Cienfuegos will be there with some other Cubans and their wives. This will be our best chance to eliminate him. We also believe he will use this opportunity to meet with his Peruvian contact. I am going to let my colleagues fill you in on his habits and the various methods we have worked out on how you may best approach him. You will be there as Mexican honeymooners. We will get you to Acapulco by boat and then by train to the Yucatan. Your cover story is in the folders. Study it. You are booked at the resort in the bridal suite."

Thorny and Myra listened and made notes on their briefing. The details were explained by the two men who did not identify themselves.

Thorny and Myra would leave on the following Saturday. Adela wished them luck. It was all very precise and professional. It was on the way back to their apartment that Thorny started sweating and feeling ill. Once inside their home he fell into their plush sofa overlooking the gray sea.

"Myra," he said. "Are you sure about this? This is a very complicated mission that they are sending us on. And why us? It seems that it would be easier to use their own people."

"Relax, Thorny. Peru wasn't invited to this shinding. Come on; a week at a new luxury resort. Sounds good to me."

"Have you ever done a foreigner before? Wasn't most of your work done against mob guys?"

"Let's not go down memory lane here. You just do what I say and we will be fine. Adela and her team were very thorough. I can do this. Plus we get a free vacation."

"I'm glad you're so at ease with this. This is some change from following cheating husbands."

"Oh shut up and give me a kiss. Here is where we make our bones as a team. This is going to lead to big paydays. I've got plans for us. Let's get some food and I will lay it all out for you. I hope you didn't think that I was going to spend the rest of my days being front man for these backwater coke dealers."

"Coke dealers? What the hell are you talking about?"

"You blind, Thorny? What do you think fuels this economy? Don't you remember that tea we drank in Cuzco? The tea made from coca leaves? It ain't llama wool and tater tots that are keeping these fat cats in their haciendas. The Shining Path creeps may scream about democracy and helping the poor but all they really want is to get their hands on the cocaine cash."

"I thought the drug shit came from Mexico."

"Some of it does but the raw material is processed here and then run up through the Bahamas. Peru and Bolivia are coca central. We could probably grab a piece of the action if we wanted to but drugs are not my thing. I don't like them and it seems you don't either."

"You got that right. I've seen what they can do to people. Look what happened to Chet Baker, Art Pepper, Gerry and Charlie Parker. These men are musical gods. I'll stick to beer and some single malt. OK, let's get some food and you can lay it all out to me. Right now I'm a nervous wreck. It all seemed fun and games until I realized what they are asking of us. I don't have the nerve that you do."

Myra took Thorny into her arms. "Relax. When this Indian goes on the warpath then the white man better watch out."

TWENTY-TWO

The glowing dial on the clock said 2:49. Thorny sat on the balcony drinking a beer. Myra was asleep. After a quick dinner they had spent the rest of the evening going over the material Adela and her agent's had given them. They both now had brand new Mexican passports. They kept the names given them when they had left Canada. Jose and Maria Cardenas were their names.

Because of Mexico's strict gun rules the Peruvian's had chosen poison as the means of assassination. Myra was listed as a diabetic. She had a case with a number of needles and a set of Insulin bottles. They were filled with a deadly poison made by natives in the Amazonian jungle. One injection and death came quickly. How they would get close enough to the target was going to be the problem.

Thorny had no doubts that Myra was more than capable of doing the deed. Never the less he was worried. He doubted anyone would think he was a Mexican. His Spanish was now very good but many of the idioms still escaped him. He would have to remain in the background or pretend he was a mute. Luckily he knew enough ASL to get by. He had learned it from a deaf pal in high school.

The briny smell of the sea floated up to where he was seated. The dim light from the semi-functioning street lights cast an orange glow over the damp, deserted streets. He knew sleep was not going to come. He was too wound up. He had always considered himself to be a cool guy but Myra made him look like Don Knotts on speed. She seemed to take everything in stride. There was a calm competency that seemed to spill off of her. It was a new sensation for him to be this dependant on a woman. He had always set the rules and the limits to his relationships. He was now the junior partner in an enterprise that he still had his doubts about. Myra seemed to trust Adela and the agency she worked within but Thorny had his questions. If they became a burden then their elimination would be easy. Officially they no longer existed. It was almost as if they were living on quicksand. The footing was slippery and liable to give way at any moment. Thorny missed the Chicago streets. Lukes beef and sausage. Due's pizza. Dog & Suds, Carmens, and all his other hangouts. The jazz or what they called jazz was dismal in Lima. The excitement of the new digs and the new life was starting to wear off. He was not sure the price they had to pay to get away from Lemmy was worth it. He was sure he was in love with Myra but the more he thought about it the more he wondered if the need to escape was more for her benefit than his. He could have just quit on Bats. He did not have to be the guy to take the fall for Lemmy's shit. But here he was. From a semi bent P.I. to an international assassin. Maybe if things did not go well in Cancun he could convince Myra to split from the whole deal. But where the hell would they go? They would have both Lemmy and the Peruvian CIA after them. Where would they be safe? Maybe plastic surgery. But they had little money. Myra had given Adela the drug money. It bought them a safe place to hide but now they were obliged to perform hits for their bread. They had a nice life but it could be taken away any time the Peruvians decided they were no longer needed. Myra counted on Adela's friendship but she wasn't in control. And while they had not seen Colonel Navarett since they were in Vancouver, Thorny knew he was against using them. Something could happen to Adela and they would be without any help. The whole situation seemed very precarious to Thorny. He was surprised that Myra did not give it a thought. She had enough self confidence for them both. Maybe it came from being an outsider. How many black Indians were there?

A cat howled in the night. A man on a bycicle rolled by under the balcony. Thorny shook his head. Well, he thought, if nothing else I'll have some great stories to tell my grandkids.

He let out a laugh. As if he would ever have grandkids. If he was sure about one thing it was that Myra lacked any maternal urges. He closed the balcony doors and crawled back into bed.

Ready or not, he whispered to no one; Mexico, here we come.

TWENTY-THREE

They were into their third day at the resort. They had barely caught a glimpse of the Cubans. They were being housed on a separate floor and wing of the luxury resort. It wasn't until the morning of the fourth day that they finally caught a glimpse of the Cubans. The day was overcast. It was hot and humid. The Cuban group had taken over a large cabana by the deep end of the hotel's pool. Myra strolled by them in her tiny pink bikini. Every eye followed her movements. Cienfuego's was doing laps in the huge pool. Discreet guards watched over him. As he neared the edge of the pool, Myra suddenly dove into the water. She came close to hitting the Cuban official. He came up sputtering.

"What are you doing?" he asked in heavily accented Cuban Spanish. "You stupid woman. You nearly hit me."

Myra popped up beside the man. "Oh, I am so sorry. I did not see you. I must apologize."

Myra pulled herself out of the pool. Cienfuego's watched her like a vulture about to swoop in on its prey. He smiled up at her.

"Ah, it is of no matter," he said. "Are you staying here at the hotel?"

Thorny sat nearby and could hear them but had trouble catching all the words. The Cuban spoke a rapid fire Spanish that was filled with idioms. Myra, luckily, had no trouble.

"Yes, I am," she said. She sat on the edge of the pool drying her hair. The Cuban could not take his eyes off of her. And he was not the only one who was admiring her figure. Even the other Cuban women were staring.

Cienfuegos came out of the water. "Please allow me to introduce myself. I am Antonio Cienfuegos. I and my friends are here to enjoy the sea and the sun. I take it you are Mexican?"

"Is that a problem?"

"Not at all. But as you are then perhaps you can introduce us to the pleasures of your country. The food in the hotel leaves much to be desired. And may I have the pleasure of learning your name?"

"Senora Maria Cardenas. That is my poor husband over there."

Myra pointed at Thorny. He was playing his role as the bored and dejected husband.

"Well then you may both be my guests. Do you know of a suitable place to dine that features more adventuresome fare than we have found in this less than desirable hotel?"

"Oh yes, I do. There is a lovely place that features a very creative chef. She uses only local ingredients but does magic with them."

"That sounds delightful. And what brings you here? Vacation or work."

"Neither," Myra said with a look of disgust on her face. "This is supposed to be my honeymoon. But I fear I may have made a mistake. Look at him pouting over there. As long as we were living in Ciudad Mexico, living with his mother, he was fine. Away from her and he seems lost. Oh, I should not be sharing all this with a stranger like you but I am so mad. Money makes fools of us all. I am not sure I can pay the price for the luxurious life I thought I was entitled to. Better to go back working at the dress shop."

The Cuban rested a hand on Myra's knee. "No need to be sad. You are much too beautiful to wear such a frown. Perhaps it would do your new husband good to realize what he has and what he may lose. Come out with me tonight. You can show me the sights and I will show you what real men are capable of with a woman such as you."

Myra removed the Cuban's hand from her knee. "You presume much, Sir. I am a married woman. Being unhappy is not an excuse to behave in an improper manner. From your accent I would presume you are Puerto Rican. Is that so?"

"That is very astute of you, Maria," the Cuban lied.

"Oh, I have heard what rascals you Puerto Ricans are. I am not sure that I trust your intentions."

"I believe that you know full well what my intentions are. I also believe that you are too much of a woman to be bound by convention and a husband who still seems in need of diapers. Tell me I am wrong."

"To do that would be to lie. I will some how find a way to sneak out tonight. Tell me your room number. I will meet you there and we can escape out the back way. Can you have a car waiting?"

"Anything can be arranged. I am in room 1936. Call when you can get free. You can not come to my room. I am being watched as we all are."

Myra gave the dark haired man a quizzical look. "Whatever do you mean? Are you a criminal? What am I doing talking to you?"

"No, it is nothing to worry about. It is just that we are in a foreign country and my associates all look out for each other."

"If that is the case then we must part now for they are watching us. I will call."

Myra wrapped herself in a large beach towel and walked away. She slapped Thorny in the head. He jumped up and followed her into the hotel lobby. The Cuban stared at her swaying backside with a huge grin on his face. He just hoped that none of the other party lackeys would have the nerve to question his chatting up the Mexican. They had all been told to stay away from any locals. The party was very paranoid of any CIA activity. But Cienfuegos was the senior official and held power over the rest of his staff. He could not wait to get his hands on the luscious Mexican newlywed. He would have to find another hotel to take her to. He could not risk any prying eyes.

He joined his staff at the cabana.

"Who is that woman?" the wife of his assistant asked.

Cienfuegos laughed. "Can you believe how stupid these Mexicans are? She thought I was Puerto Rican. I played along and told her tall tales of my home land. No wonder Mexico wallows in the mud of the Yankee pigs. They are a people without honor. It is good to see what depths the rest of the Latin American world will sink to just to have a seat at the foot of the American table. You are all lucky to live in the time of Fidel. He has saved your souls from the evil corruption of capitalism. Now come, we must work on our presentation for when we return. I have calls to make and will not join you tonight. Tomorrow, after breakfast, we will meet in the conference room at eleven. I want everything thing worked out by then. The plan for the bridges and roads must be done for when we return to Havana. Now get moving."

TWENTY-FOUR

Thorny awoke to find he was all alone in the huge bed that dominated their hotel suite. Myra had refused to allow him to go with her on her dinner date with the Cuban. He was unsure just what to do. He arose from the bed as the telephone rang. He gingerly picked it up. He was afraid what he might hear. He moved it slowly to his ear. He waited.

"Downstairs. Breakfast room. Fifteen minutes."

It was Myra. Before he could say a word the connection was closed. He dressed as fast as possible. He splashed his face with tepid water. He combed his hair. Was she in trouble? Had something happened that upset her plans? He left the room and ran to the elevator. He stood nervously shifting from one foot to the other. The elevator arrived. The doors slid open in an agonizingly slow manner. He stood as rigid as a statue as it descended. The lobby had people scurrying to and fro. He spotted the Cubans gathered in a corner. He did not see Cienfuegos among them. They were all chattering away. He walked past them and entered the restaurant. He did not see Myra and began to panic. A woman at the back of the restaurant waved at him. She had bright red hair and wore outlandishly huge sunglasses. He sighed and walked calmly to her table. It was Myra in one of her disguises.

"Jesus, you had me worried. Where were you all night? What happened?"

She looked around to make sure no one was in hearing distance.

"The job is done. It took some time to get the contracted locals to take control of the package. It was best to not be seen anywhere near our hotel so I did not return until this morning."

"So our mission is accomplished? We can leave now? Those other Cubans are going crazy in the lobby. They must know he is missing."

"That is not the problem. Getting rid of that pig was the easy part. We have another problem."

Thorny's heart skipped a beat. Whatever he thought he was back in Chicago he now realized that being an assassin was not his cup of tea. He could not understand how Myra could be so cool. Simply talking about what she had done was getting him all sweaty. He could feel his stomach knotting up.

"Then just what is our problem?"

"It was at dinner. The Cuban wanted to take me to a club to meet someone. He said it was unexpected business that would only take a short time and then he said he had a place for us to go. He wanted to take me to Tres Flechas. It is a disco. I decided to end things there. When we left the restaurant I gave him the shot. Our team was waiting. They got him into a car and left. I wanted to see who he was going to meet at the disco. I thought this might be valuable information for Adela. Luckily I put on this wig and glasses. The Cuban told me that he had a private room reserved at the disco. When I got there I asked to be shown the room where the meeting was to take place. The hostess pointed to a door at the top of a staircase. The noise in the place was deafening. I went upstairs. I stopped a waitress and asked her to go inside and see if anyone was there yet. When she opened the door is when our problems started."

"What do you mean?"

"I peeked over her shoulder. Seated at a table was our own Colonel Navarett."

"What? You mean he's working with the Cubans?"

"I don't know. What I do know is that we have to get back to Lima and talk to Adela. They will never find the Cubans body. That is for certain. But why was the Colonel meeting with the Cuban? We have to leave immediately. I want you to go upstairs and pack everything. Go out the back. I have a car there. Just to be safe we will drive to Oaxaca and get a plane from there. Now go and hurry. I'll be waiting. Do not bother to check out."

Thorny did as he was told. Once back in the room he packed everything. He wiped down everything he had touched. He was probably being over cautious but old habits die hard. He went down the stairs and out a back door next to the kitchen. No one paid any attention to him. He saw a black Toyota sitting at the end of the alleyway. Myra, still in disguise was seat behind the wheel. He put their bags in the trunk. He climbed in. She drove to the main street.

"One thing I have learned in this business is that nothing ever goes as planned. I never liked that bastard but I never figured him for a traitor."

"Whoa there, Myra. Maybe it was official business. We don't know what the status is between Peru and Cuba. Maybe it was some back channel negotiation. Maybe he didn't know you were there to off the Cuban."

"Bullshit; he knew. Do you think Adela sets these things up on her own? We will just have to wait until we see her. I can't risk calling and talking on an open phone line. I may have to but it is risky. You never know who is listening or if they have all the international lines tapped. We will be back home by tonight and then we will see what happens next."

"Christ, do I miss Chicago. I want to be with you, Myra but I don't know if I am cut out for this. And wait a minute. If the Colonel knew we were coming to kill the Cuban then why didn't he warn him about us? This is not making any sense. Was the Colonel alone at the disco? Was there anyone else there?"

"Cowboy up, Thorny. I'm doing the work. You have nothing to worry about. Come on, where you going to get this kind of juice? What, you want to sit around the yard, mow the grass, and watch TV? Don't be a drag. Plus you wait until we get back to Lima. At the end of a job I get fired up. Hot and horny. Look at it this way; I do the work and you reap the benefits. Now lighten up and let's get home. Adela will have some answers. And I really don't like to know any more than I need to in order to do the job. I could care less what the Colonel is up to. I am just a hired gun. I leave all the political crap to those that care. I'll inform Adela because she is a friend but what she does with the info is not my concern. Getting involved in that kind of shit leads to trouble.

Now lighten up. Jobs over. Time for some fun."

Myra reached over and grabbed Thorny's crotch. She started laughing. Thorny had to join her despite his misgivings.

TWENTY-FIVE

Thorny sat in the passenger seat of the rented car. They were somewhere between Acapulco and Oaxaca. Myra had stopped to call Adela. She was now unsure about flying back to Lima. For all she knew Adela might have been removed and we would be walking into a trap. They had stopped in a small dusty village in search of a phone. She was using a local phone in a small roadside cantina that they had stopped at. Thorny was on the verge of falling asleep after downing two cold beers. He turned in his seat to see Myra come running back to the car. She flung open the door and jumped in.

"We have a problem. When I called Adela I got an answering machine."

"What was the message? Maybe she is out."

"It isn't what was on the message; it was who was not on it."

"What do you mean?"

"Adela and I have codes. All I heard were 3 beeps. That means everything is scrapped. Move to plan B."

"What the hell is plan B?"

"Basically it means everything has gone wrong and we are on our own."

"On our own? What the hell does that mean?"

"Just what I said. Give me a second to think. This must have something to do with the Colonel. But that doesn't matter. We have to get out of Mexico."

"Where are we going? Where can we go?"

"Back to Chicago."

"Are you crazy, Myra? They are looking for us there. Lemmy will have the city all over us the minute we land at O'Hare."

"No choice. We need operating money and that is where it is."

"What money? I thought we gave all the drug money to the Peruvians for our escape."

"We did but that is not what I'm talking about. I'll make it brief. We have to get going. A while ago I did a job for Lemmy. It was maybe 3 years back. I had to off a drug guy who was moving on Lemmy's territory. After I did the creep I searched his place. It was out in McHenry County; a summer place. I searched the house figuring that there might be some drugs I could either sell or use for more leverage with Lemmy. What I found was a gym bag with half a mil in it. I have it in a safety deposit box at Lincoln National Bank. Joey Gabs asked me if I found anything at the guy's hideout. I told him to tell Lemmy that I found nothing."

"Wait a second, Myra. If you thought we were running to Peru with the odds being that we would never return to the US then why didn't you just get the money out and bring it with us?"

"Just for cases like this. I figured we would be away for a few years at the most. I never thought we would never return. So we are coming back a little early. But not to worry. We will enter the states as Mexican citizens on vacation. I'll wear my wig and we can fake you up once we get back to the city. All we have to do is get to the bank. I have other ID's there and other passports. I got a guy who will fix you up. We take the cash and head for the Greek Islands or Portugal or somewhere else."

"But what about Adela and the Colonel and the Cubans?"

"Not our problem. I'm more worried about Lemmy. The mob has people all over the world. If he is pissed enough we will always be looking over our shoulder."

"So, what can we do?"

"Take him out."

"What? Are you nuts? And how do you propose to do that? He never goes anywhere alone. You told me that. He always has his goons around him."

"Let me worry about that. Do you think I've lasted this long because I don't know what I'm doing? That fat fuck needs taking out. First my Pops and then me been doing his shit for a long time. That half a mil will set us up and I want a nice long rest. I thought going off to Peru would be fun. But, you know schwat? I'm getting tired of this shit. I would like, even for a while, to live like a normal person. Have a house, cook a dinner. I don't want to live that half life where I am only biding time between calls from Lemmy;s flunkies. Plus, sooner or later, I will screw up and either end up dead or in the joint for a long, long time. So what do you say, Thorny? You coming with me or you got something better to do?"

I smiled at her. I shook my head.

"Yo no tiene nada ahora; solamente Usted."

Myra laughed. "Si, es verdad."

TWENTY-SIX

The customs agent at O'Hare Airport hardly gave them a second glance. A worn out and exhausted pair of fugitives dragged themselves outside the terminal. A long taxi drive delivered them to Union Station in downtown Chicago. Myra wore her blonde wig. Thorny was in sunglasses, a fake moustache, and a long raincoat. They sat calmly, bone tired, but safe so far. Thorny was still on edge, Myra seemed her usual calm and cool self. Thorny fidgeted in place.

"Relax, will you," whispered Myra. "No one is looking for two Mexican tourists. Did you make that call?"

Thorny turned to her. His heart still missed a beat every time he looked into her coal black eyes. All he could think of was the word smitten. Or maybe it should be bitten. Once she sank her fangs into his heart, he had become a slave just like Dracula's victims.

"No problem. Stippy has the coach house all ready for us. But won't we need wheels?"

"Don't worry about that. Boosting cars was one of the first things that Rufus taught me. But we may not have to worry about that. Leave it to me. I just want to get some place we can have a bath, some food, and a few days sleep. And you need to calm down. I told you I know what I'm doing."

"Jesus, you are something. How can you stay so cool? Do you realize we are now international fugitives on the run?"

"Yeah, and you saw how easy it was to get into the country. Most of these cops couldn't find their own dicks with a road map. Shit, you should know that. You've been dealing with these dimwits for years."

"Agreed but even a cop gets lucky sometime."

"Don't worry about the cops. We aren't even on their radar. It's the mob assholes that we have to avoid."

Myra checked her watch. "Let's go. Our train is arriving."

Once on the train both Myra and Thorny fell into a troubled sleep. Their route out of Mexico had been full of stops and starts. They had been awake for over two days. Thorny had slipped the conductor a ten spot and told him to wake them at the Lake Forest stop. Stippy, hopefully, would be waiting for them.

Despite being bone tired, Thorny awoke when he felt the train slowing down. He poked Myra. She opened her eyes and smiled.

"I was dreaming of a beach on Maui," she said. "We'll get there yet."

"I sure hope so. Meanwhile, a bed and some food will have to do."

The train pulled into the station. They climbed down to an empty platform. Waiting in the station house was the rotund Stippy. He waved.

Thorny smiled when Stippy strode up and embraced him.

"You are safe," Stippy said. "Come with me. Berta is waiting."

Stippy hardly glanced at Myra. Thorny knew that Stippy blamed all his problems on her. He didn't know that she had probably saved his life by warning him about Bats betrayal. Thorny would straighten him out later. Right now he just wanted to get them all somewhere safe. They needed food and sleep.

* *

Thorny sat on the edge of the bed in the coach house. Myra was taking a shower. Stippy stood over him.

"We are przyjaciele, rodacy, but you are zwariovaney," Stippy said.

Myra, wrapped in a towel, emerged from the bathroom. She was smiling. Her hair was wrapped in a pink towel.

"What did he say?" she asked Thorny.

"He said that we are friends, countrymen but that I am crazy."

She turned to Stippy. "Do you think he is crazy for being with me?"

"Ah, this boy was always crazy. But I must be honest. This is crazy even for him. Berta and I, we are like family to Thorny. And now he is off to South America, to

Mexico, Lemmy is after you both. You want to tell me that this is not crazy. Maybe you are safe here but maybe not. I am known. People talk. You can't hide here forever. What are you going to do>"

"Well, as soon as you leave, I am going to dry off and go to sleep. We can talk later. Do not worry Stippy, like I told Thorny, I know what I am doing. All I need is a little time. I have a plan. We will be fine. You and Berta just go on as if we are not here. All I need is a few days. Will that be OK?"

Stippy shook his head. He muttered in Polish under his breath. "Yes, that is fine. You both sleep. I will return after we close tonight. Do not put on any lights."

Stippy turned and left. Myra dropped her towel. She turned to Thorny. "You're turn in the shower. I'll be waiting."

"Are you kidding? I'm ready to faint and you want to get it on?"

"Sure; why not. Being exhausted makes me horny. Hurry up or I'll have to take care of myself. You can watch if you want but I think something else might be better for the both of us."

Myra laughed and threw herself on the bed. "Hurry up, Thorny."

Thorny, despite his aching bones, did as he was told.

PART THREE

TWENTY-SEVEN

"Shit, Thorny," said Billy Little. "Don't get me wrong. I mean me and the guys are really happy for what you're doing for us. That gig at the Green Mill was winding down and it seemed like whatever momentum we had going for us was dying on the vine. Stippy asked around but nothing was happening. Then you come along and things started taking off. That is really cool. But I gotta' ask, you know, just between me and you, what gives? It's like you vanish for months with that dame and then boom! You show up looking all different. I mean; blonde hair and that womb broom? I can dig it but it is a little strange. And then all of a sudden things start popping for us. I thought you were a private investigator. So, you tell me. How come all of a sudden we are floating in cash, bookings, record deals and you stop with the P.I. gig and become a band manager? I mean, you gotta' know, we all got questions. I don't want to look a gift horse in the mouth or queer things but this is one strange happening. I'm sure you got your reasons but me and the guys are wondering if we are walking into something that might come back to bite us on the ass. I know what happens to guys who get owned by criminals. Maybe if you're Frank Sinatra it works OK but five black guys ain't gonna' be so lucky is what we figure. So if you can lay something on me to set our minds at ease it would be a big help."

Thorny looked up at Billy. He sighed. Maybe it was time to level with the band. But what could he say that would not drag them into the shit?

"Listen to me, Billy," Thorny said in a soft voice. "You are correct. Don't look into that horse's mouth. You have nothing to worry about. Everything we do, every step we make, every contract we sign is on the up and up. No criminal element here. You stick to writing and rehearsing. We have that showcase coming up in New York. The more offers we get, the better the deal I can finagle. We have interest from Blue Note and a few other labels but I want to get the best deal I can for you guys. So don't sweat where the money or the push is coming from. Everything is legit. But I think our time in Chicago is over. The action is on the coasts."

Billy shook his head. "Sure, I believe you but still something don't seem right."

"Fine, Billy. You guys go find someone else. I'll cancel the showcase. I'll cancel the tour dates. I'll tell the record companies that you guys are not interested anymore. You can go back to playing for chump change and keeping the day jobs. Be my guest. I didn't need to do this. I'm a fan and just wanted to help out. We haven't signed anything yet. Just say the word and I'm gone."

"Whoa, Thorny. Ease up. Jesus, don't you think we got a right to be suspicious? I mean you come out of nowhere and suddenly you're the manager doing all sorts of stuff. Never mind about what I said. I mean I know this is a big chance and maybe we're just a little scared. You don't get many shots in this business and we sure don't want to queer the deal. Forget I said anything.

We'll see you next week. We'll be ready to head out of town. Meantime we have to rehearse the new material and get ready for the big trip east."

"Great. Leave everything else to me. I'm going to LA for the weekend. I need to pick a guy's brain about a couple of things. You just keep the other guys working and then it's off to New York week after next."

Thorny watched as Billy went trough the revolving doors at The Artists Café. He watched as Billy descended the steps to the subway. Maybe Billy was right, he thought. What am I doing? But why ask stupid questions? He just wanted to get out of town. After what had gone down Chicago was no longer a safe place for him. Maybe he wasn't on the Mob's radar. Lemmy was dead and the word was that Myra was the shooter. But sooner or later he would be. He knew he should have never returned from Milwaukee but he thought he was safe at least for awhile. He stared out the window at the passing parade on Michigan Avenue. Business men in suits walked by as if they were on their way to save the world. Office girls in their short skirts and high heels rushed back from lunch or shopping. Students hustling to class wove in and out of the human traffic. Without realizing it was happening tears began streaming down Thorny's face. He dabbed at his cheeks with a soiled napkin.

"Sweetie, you OK?" asked the passing waitress.

Thorny looked up into the sad tired eyes of an older woman adorned in pink. He forced a smile.

"Sure, Doris. Just a memory."

"Must be some sad memory. I'm going to bring you a piece of apple pie and a scoop. Maybe cheer you up, kiddo. We don't want no sad faces here."

She grinned. She reached out and pinched Thorny's cheek. But it was no help. Thorny, despite his best efforts could not stop from recalling the horrors of the past few weeks.

TWENTY-EIGHT

They sat at a back table. It was hidden from the front door. The place was bathed in the dim glow of a slowly fading afternoon as it shone through the dirt caked across the front window. It was a drinking man's bar and, at this time of day, the men were working. At 4 in the afternoon they were the only ones in the place. The White Eagle was owned by Len Sobieski who was a pal of Stippy's. They felt safe here. No self respecting hoodlum would be caught dead in a place like this. But taking no chances they were still in disguise. Myra was now a redhead in a tan raincoat sporting oversized sunglasses. She had gotten Thorny into a blond wig, paste-on moustache, and horn-rimmed specs. They did not want to be recognized by anyone.

"But how in the hell are you going to get close enough to Lemmy to shoot him?"

"I'm not sure," Myra said. "Even in this get up I'll be recognized. I can get his attention but you may have to do it."

"Are you kidding? How am I going to get that close to him?"

"I'm thinking our best bet is when he goes to Papa Milano's. He's there every Sunday night. He sits in the kitchen with a pair of goomba's standing watch over his fat ass. I walk in and surprise him. You come in the back and make sure we have a safe exit. I'll take care of the greaseballs and Lemmy. Then we take off."

"Why don't we just take the money you have and get out of here now?"

"Because if he knows I'm still alive then we will never be safe. I'm sure that fuck Butch told him how we ripped off the truck. Plus when I killed Joey Gabs, I killed one of his prime earners. This is the way it has to be. Once Lemmy is dead then the rest of these scumbags will be offing each other left and right to try and take over the city. They won't be giving a thought to me. Luckily they don't know who you are or what you look like. There's a back door to the kitchen from off the alley at Milano's. It should be easy for you to get inside unless Lemmy's gotten more paranoid and puts somebody in the alley. If that's the case then you are going to have to deal with whoever is out there."

"How do you know about a back door in the alley?"

"Because it is part of what I do. Anywhere that I might have to pull off a hit has to be fully checked out. Part of being a successful button man is to have a second and third avenue of escape. You know; best laid plans and all that."

"Yeah, I guess so. But Jesus, Myra. I can't wrap my head around the idea that we are going to off the head of the Chicago mob. You sure think a lot bigger than me."

"Think big or go home. Sure we could just take off like you want but that leaves unfinished business. Rufus taught me to never leave anything to chance. It will always return to bite you. We have a couple of days to figure things out. Leave it to me. Let's drink up and head out to Highwood. I need sleep and time to think."

"Think about what, Myra? It seems pretty cut and dried. You shoot the guards and I'll come in the back door and keep watch. Seems simple enough. You boost a car. We leave it nearby. We do the deed. We take off. Ditch the car. Head up to Milwaukee. Catch a plane to some where and that's it."

"Sounds reasonable to me. But we can't take a chance of leaving our documents and cash in a stolen car. We will have to put everything in money belts and have it on us."

"Why? Stippy can store everything in his safe. We just pick the stuff up on our way out of town."

"No. That leaves too many moving parts. Plus if anything goes south you put Stippy in the middle of things. Let's do things my way. I'm the professional. I've trained my whole life for this. You just have to trust me. Remember, I saved your scrawny body and got us this far. Just a few more days and we will be in the clear. Now let's get going."

Once again Thorny got that unhinged feeling. It was that knot in the pit of his stomach that took his breath away. It wasn't fear exactly but something close to it. It was as if he were caught in a spider web. No matter what he did, it just entangled him more and more. He stood up and started swaying. Myra caught him by the arm.

"Jesus Thorny, this is no time to be getting panic attacks. Stay cool. It'll be a breeze. Even if Butch spilled to Lemmy, he probably thinks we are long gone. He would never figure us to be here. He probably has guys in Vegas or California looking for us. He knows I like it in those places."

"How would he know that?"

"I once told Joey Gabs about it. I was going to move there but he put the brakes on that. He told me that Lemmy nixed the move. He wanted me close by. But that was years ago. But he never forgets things like that."

"Does he know about Peru and what you did there?"

"No. I'm pretty sure he never glommed on to that deal. He thought I was in Europe taking some time off."

"I still don't understand how you ended up working for the Peruvian CIA. One of these days you are going to have to tell me the story."

"Sure, Thorny. I'll do it over margarita's on the Spanish Riviera or in the Black Forest or floating down the Danube. There are so many beautiful places in Europe where we can just disappear."

"I did always want to see Paris."

"No problemo. You won't believe the food there. And the jazz is great. So many players who got fed up with the Jim Crow shit here are over there. You know that, I'm sure."

Thorny smiled at the thought despite the fog of fear that hung on him like a shroud. It would be great to see Dexter Gordon again.

They left a big tip for Len. He simply nodded and said nothing. They went out the front door. The sky had faded from a dim glow to an overcast gray. Thorny looked up. The weather matched his mood. They headed for the raggedy Plymouth that Myra had stolen.

Once inside the car Thorny stared at Myra. He could not shake that lump in the pit of his stomach. His mother had believed in evil omens and bad signs. Maybe she had been on to something. Myra was smiling.

Nothing seemed to bother her. Thorny heaved a huge sigh. They headed north as the sky opened and a heavy rain started to fall. Myra turned on the cars radio. Blasting out was Cozy Cole's latest. Maybe that was an omen. But an omen of what?

TWENTY-NINE

Thorny parked the newly stolen DeSoto three blocks away from Rush Street. Its faded paint and salt-rusted body would not draw any attention. He walked towards Milano's. Dusk had fallen. The streets did not have much foot traffic. He walked past the front of the restaurant. He spotted Myra sitting in the window of the bar across the street. She was still in the red wig. He continued to the next block. Thorny shivered. The night had turned cool. Turning down the side street, he entered the alley at the back of Milano's. It smelled of rotted food and garlic. Steam came from the restaurants vents. Garbage littered the cracked concrete. A man in an overcoat leaned against the back door that led to the kitchen. He was smoking a cigarette. Thorny hesitated. He fingered the sap that weighed down his coat pocket. He walked briskly towards the man. As the man pushed himself off the wall and turned towards Thorny he was met with the lead-weighted sap across his forehead. He started to stagger forward. Thorny hit him as hard as he could on top of the head. The man crumpled at Thorny's feet. Thorny hit him once again across his temple. He was out cold if not dead. Thorny glanced up and down the alley. He saw no one. He rolled the man over and searched him. He pulled a .38 from his inside pocket. It went into Thorny's coat. He removed the unconscious mans wallet and took all the cash that it held. He put the wallet in another pocket. He dragged the man behind one of the refuse containers that stood alongside the back door entrance. He looked at his watch. Myra should be entering the restaurant now. He took a deep breath and opened the door to the kitchen.

It was busy and steamy inside. He spotted two men standing on either side of the door leading to the private dining room that Lemmy used. Before the men spotted Thorny, Myra appeared. There were two soft sputterings from the huge pistol that Myra held in her hand. The two men crumpled silently to the floor. Myra walked up to the crumpled bodies. She sent another bullet into the heads of each man. Everything in the kitchen came to a stand still. Myra waved her pistol and gestured towards the back door. The cooks and waiters took the hint and headed out into the alley. Thorny came up alongside Myra. She nodded at him. He nodded back. He knocked on the door. A voice from inside said, "What?"

"Phone for the boss."

The door cracked open. "Who the hell are you?"

Myra's pistol popped again and the man's head exploded. Thorny tried to kick open the door but the man had fallen against it. Shots rang out splintering the door. Myra and Thorny stood on either side of the door. They looked at each other. Time was running out. Any minute someone from out front would be here to see where all the servers were.

Myra lit a towel from the stove and threw it into the room that Lemmy was in. Then she lit and threw another. More shots came from inside. Thorny turned to the swinging doors that led to the main dining room. A large man in a tuxedo started to enter the kitchen. Thorny yelled for him to stay away. His face went white. He looked at the gun in Thorny's hand. He turned and left. Thorny motioned for Myra to step to the side. He threw himself against the door. It crashed open. Both Lemmy and his bodyguard started shooting. Myra peeked around the door and fired quickly. The bodyguard's face erupted like a volcano spewing red lava. He went down in a crumpled heap. Lemmy, holding a pistol in both hands, fired a quick succession of shots. Thorny pulled the gun from his pocket and fired. Lemmy went down. Thorny leapt off the floor.

"Let's get out of here," he shouted. He turned. Myra was lying on her side on the floor. She was holding her arm to her side and moaning. Blood was gushing out of her. Thorny lifted her up. He grabbed another towel as he pushed her towards the back door. He opened it. The staff had scattered. He half carried and half walked Myra towards the waiting car. She kept slipping in and out of consciousness. He only hoped that they could make it there before the cops showed up. Myra was moaning but much softer. She could barely stay upright. Some passing people stopped and stared. Thorny smiled.

"Drunk again." he said to the staring pedestrians.

They finally got to the car. The sound of police sirens began to fill the air. Thorny got Myra inside. The bleeding seemed to have lessened. He drove them west. He didn't want to involve Stippy in this but he did not know where else to go. Thorny looked over at the slumped Myra. Her red wig had fallen off. Her black hair was pinned up. She had passed out. Thorny drove on into the darkness that had fallen. His heart was beating so hard he was afraid his chest would explode.

THIRTY

Thorny pulled the car into Stippy's driveway and parked behind the restaurant. Myra was not moving. Stippy and Berta came running out of the bar. Luckily the club was dark this Sunday and only a few people were inside drinking at the bar. Without a word they carried the unconscious Myra upstairs to the coach house.

"What the hell happened," asked Stippy.

"She did it," answered Thorny. "She killed them all. But Lemmy shot her. I killed him. I think I killed him. We didn't hang around to find out. Do you know a doctor? She looks bad."

Berta was tending to Myra. When she lifted her to remove her blouse, a river of blood came running out of her side. She was white as a sheet. Berta was trying to stem the flow of blood but with little success. Berta turned to Stippy.

"Call Herman. Call him now. This is bad; very bad."

Stippy went to the phone. Thorny stood frozen. Berta looked up at him and shook her head. She felt for a pulse in Myra's neck. She looked at Thorny once more. The look on her face told him all he needed to know. Stippy closed the phone.

"Herman is on his way. He was a medic in the old country. He will know what to do."

Berta stood up. "It is too late. She is gone. I'm sorry Thorny but we must remove her now."

Thorny was frozen. He stared at Myra's lifeless form. Berta was cutting away Myra's blouse. She removed the thick money belt from her waist. It was covered in blood.

"Take this Thorny. You have to leave. I'm sorry but it is better if Herman does not see you. We will tell him that Myra was killed during an argument in the club. Say your goodbye. We have to protect ourselves. If you care about us you must get far away."

Berta handed Thorny the money belt. She hugged him and kissed him on both cheeks.

"Oh my boy; what have you done? For our sakes please do not come back or contact us. This is very bad. Bad for you and bad for us. You should have never brought her here."

Stippy came and hugged Thorny. "Take the car and dump it somewhere. You must go now. I'm sorry, Thorny. We have helped all we can. Powodzenia, przyjacielu."

Thorny ran out the door. He did not want to think or feel. He hurried to the car. In seconds he was heading west towards the highway. He raced into the night driving north to Wisconsin.

He drove in a daze. He forced himself to think of nothing but getting rid of the stolen car he was in. He drove into the industrial part of Milwaukee. He was looking for an auto junkyard. He found one in a run down area of the city. He pulled into an alley that ran along the back of the junk yard. He had been wearing gloves so that he would leave no prints. Standing in the dark, he put Myra's money belt around his waist adding it to the one he was already wearing. He pulled his suitcase out of the back seat. He started walking. He found a gas station that was still open. He called a cab and directed the driver to the Statler Hotel. Luckily his raincoat was reversible so that he could hide all the blood stains. He staggered into an empty lobby. Milwaukee was an early town especially on a Sunday night. He registered with a phony name. He gave the sleazy looking balding clerk 300 dollars as a deposit on a weeks stay. The clerk looked at him with a knowing eye. They stared at each other. The man handed Thorny a room key along with a leering smile.

"My name is Ralph," he whispered. "Call me when you need something, anything. I'll be here all night. I apologize for the lack of a bellman."

Once inside his room, Thorny fell on the bed. He was in shock. It was as if he were in a nightmare that was never going to end. He was trembling and felt very weak. He remembered that he had not eaten all day. He desperately needed a drink and some food.

"Hello, Ralph? Can you send up a ham on rye sandwich and a bottle of scotch?"

"No problem, sir. However the liquor stores are closed on Sundays. Blue laws. I do maintain my own supply and will be happy to offer you that. Is there anything else you might be in need of? I can be very resourceful for any needs you may have."

Thorny felt like throwing up. "No, just bring me the food and the bottle. And make it fast."

Thorny thought about putting a few slugs into the slimy bastard. He thought about putting a few slugs into anyone he ran into. He wanted to tear the world apart. He wanted to be on another planet. He wanted to be anywhere but where he was. For a second he thought about eating his gun. He shivered at the thought. "Jesus," he said aloud. How in the hell did I end up like this? His mind refused to function. He went from 16 frames a second to 64. Everything was racing across his mind. What the hell was he going to do now. Was he safe or not? Would anyone from the restaurant remember him? He tore off the wig and the mustache. He removed the bloody money belts. He went to his raincoat and removed the gun and his sap. He put them in a dresser drawer along with both money belts. He would deal with them later. All he wanted now was to eat something and then drink himself into oblivion. He needed to try and erase the sight of Myra lying in a pool of blood with all the life fading from her beautiful eyes.

THIRTY-ONE

Bells were ringing. Was it time for church? Was it time for his mother to dress him in his cheap suit and comb his hair for the Sunday service? No, that couldn't be. Was it that creep Ralph with his room service? He had shoved a bunch of bills in the creep's hand the first time he brought food and drink up. It was then that Thorny suddenly realized that he had removed his disguise. The sleazy bastard gave him a look that told him all he had to know. As long as Thorny kept feeding the creep money he knew the man would stay silent rather than shut off the money train. It was the telephone that was ringing. Thorny pulled open his gummy eyes. The past week spent hiding in the hotel had turned him to mush. Drinking away Myra's murder had taken its toll. He reached out and lifted the receiver from its black cradle.

"Yeah," he croaked.

"Thorny, it's Billy. Just wanted to let you know that me and the guys will be at the airport at seven tomorrow morning. We got all our arrangements and tunes locked down. This is it for us. A week at Birdland and a record deal. Man, I never thought the day would come. We'll see you in New York."

It had taken a ton of calls between Stippy, the people he knew, and Thorny wheeling and dealing on behalf of the band's future. It was his chance to get out of Chicago, the P.I. business, and most of all a chance to try and forget Myra. He would have to think about changing his name. He wanted nothing to do with his past. Just thinking about what had gone down since that strange night he first met Myra gave him chills and a knot in his stomach.

Ralph, the night clerk, had turned out to be a staunch but expensive ally in keeping Thorny half in the bag. But after a week of drinking himself to sleep he knew he had to straighten up and see that Billy and the guys were treated well. He had arranged for them to be met by the label's A&R man. They wanted to do the week at the club and try and generate some press before going into the studio. Thorny was scheduled to meet them at the studio.

After an unsteady trip to the bathroom, a quick leak and an even quicker shower Thorny rode the creaky elevator downstairs. He walked into the hotel's restaurant for breakfast. He perused the Chicago papers but found little of interest. Lemmy's murder and the shoot-out were now old news. After a third cup of coffee, he went back to his room to pack. When he had grabbed his suitcase from Stippy's coach house he did not realize that he had very little in it. His week in Milwaukee gave him a chance to get a few suits and other items. He had never before had so much money at his disposal.

Thorny put out his newly bought clothes. He started to pack. He took the money belt that Myra had worn. He emptied the remaining money. He held her true passport in his hands. He opened it to her picture. It was her without a disguise. She had others with other looks and other names. He destroyed those. He knew he should destroy the real one also but he wanted something to remember her by. He turned the belt inside out to make sure nothing remained. A receipt wrapped around a key was stuck under the zipper. He pulled it out and unfolded it. It was from a place called Grady's Storage in Janesville. It did not state what was being stored. Thorny stared at it for a long time. Could it be old furniture or family stuff that Myra wanted to save? But why would it be stored in Janesville? He looked at the receipt again. It was dated a few days before they had run to Canada.

Thorny sat down on the bed. He opened the phone and had the operator call the storage facility.

"Hello. This is Grady's Storage. You dock it and we lock it. Can I help you?"

"I hope so. I found a receipt among a relative's belongings. She passed away and I was wondering if you could tell me what she had stored in your facility."

"I wouldn't know and even if I did, I couldn't tell you. If you want to gain access you'll have to come with a death certificate and some one from law enforcement. These are self-storage units so we only collect rent and the customer provides their own form of security. Didn't you find a key or a lock combination? What is the deceased's name?"

Thorny thought fast. "No but never mind. I'll let the authorities deal with it."

Thorny hung up. He went downstairs to the front desk. He inquired as to the location of the storage place. He asked the clerk to get him a cab.

THIRTY-TWO

Thorny stood at the curb. A taxi pulled up and he got in. Thorny told the driver his destination.

"Are you kiddin' me?" asked the cabdriver. "That's over an hour away. You any idea what that will cost?"

Thorny glanced at the cab driver's license displayed on his dashboard.

"Don't worry about the cost, Manny. I'll make it worth your while."

The man stroked his chin. He looked up.

"I'll tell you what. I'm private so I can pick my fares. You throw in a lunch at the Knotty Pine and it's a deal. But you got to cover the fare round trip."

"You got it, Manny."

The drive wound its way through farm fields and a series of small towns. The ride took nearly an hour and a half. Manny pulled up to the front of a place on what appeared to be the main drag of Janesville.

"Here we are. Hope you're hungry. They got great fried chicken here. Let's eat and I'll get directions to this place you want to go."

Thorny and Manny had a delicious lunch of chicken, gravy, mashed potatoes, and green beans. Manny insisted on apple pie and ice cream. Thorny sipped at a cup of coffee. He enjoyed hearing Manny's stories of being a cabbie and some of the odd characters he had run into. Thorny revealed nothing about himself.

After paying for lunch they drove to the Storage facility. It looked to be a seedy run down place. The sign in front was hand drawn and not in a very professional manner. Thorny checked the receipt. They drove into the open lot and went down a couple of byways until they found the number of the locked roll gate on the receipt.

"Wait her, Manny. I only want to check my things. I won't be but a few minutes."

Thorny went to the gate. He inserted the key he had found into an enormous lock. It took some effort to get it open. He lifted the shuttered front and entered a large space. Sitting in the middle of the otherwise empty garage-like area was an object covered by a tan tarp. Thorny gripped the tarp and threw it off. He stepped back and smiled.

There it stood just it was that first night he had nearly been run over by Myra at its wheel. The blood red BMW shone brightly under the bare bulbs overhead. Thorny opened the driver's side door. He was assaulted with her scent. He nearly broke down in tears. He took some deep breaths. He smiled as he remembered the way she had handled the sports car. He eased into the driver's seat. A piece of paper was resting on the passenger's seat. He lifted it and opened it.

Hi Thorny. If you are reading this then I guess it all finally caught up with me. It was bound to happen sooner or later. It was a pipe dream to think I would ever escape my past. Anyway, I hope you make out. It was fun. The car is gassed up and ready to go. Remember it needs to go flat out. Try and enjoy the life you have. We had a good run. A Polack and an Indian. Who woulda' thunk it?

Myra

Thorny smiled despite the pain in his heart. He folded the note. He started up the car. It roared to life. He pulled it out of the storage room. He relocked the door. He paid Manny his round trip fare plus a huge tip. He settled back into the plush leather seats of the BMW. He intended to take Myra's advice.

Thorny shifted into first gear and took off down the road.

He had to stop and settle things at the hotel. And then it was straight to the Big Apple and a new life. Chicago would have to get along without him.

ABOUT THE AUTHOR

Steven Schwartz, originally from Chicago, now hides out in the desert southwest. He also writes under his pen name, steve shadow. All his books and stories can be found on Amazon. Signed copies of his books may be ordered from the Poisoned Pen bookstore in Scottsdale, AZ. Reviews, questions, and comments are always welcome

www.ingramcontent.com/pod-product-compliance
Lightning Source LLC
Chambersburg PA
CBHW050328160726
48002CB00001B/231